JINGLE BELL COWGIRL

LACY WILLIAMS

CHAPTER 1

*I*t was too cold today.

Lila Andrews sat in her 1970 Chevelle tapping her fingertips and rolling the lame excuse over in her mind.

It *was* cold. Cold enough that she hoped the Chevelle's temperamental engine would start back up.

She'd sat here with the engine off long enough that her breath puffed out in white clouds in front of her face. She'd always found the familiar scent of long-gone burritos and old leather soothing, but not today. Today, she could almost smell the frozen fields and pungent dried grasses across the fence.

After the long, warm autumn they'd enjoyed, winter had blasted into the small town of Redbud Trails, Oklahoma, bringing an early December ice storm that had shut down the town and left most people homebound.

It might not have been the smartest move to drive her

classic muscle car so far out of town in these conditions. But then, she had a lifetime of bad decisions behind her.

The jury was still out on whether returning to her hometown after so many years was another one.

Looking at the spread laid out before her tightened the coil in her chest. Ever since her bouts of childhood asthma, she'd imagined the tightness inside as a coil ready to spring. And boy, was it coiled tight today.

From this vantage point, parked on the side of the red dirt road on a hilltop—or what passed for one in this part of western Oklahoma—she could see a good portion of the 1,040 acre property.

The ice-blue sky arced above dried winter grasses covered in a translucent skin of ice. The pasture was one long wave of land that extended toward the horizon. She couldn't see it from here but knew that beyond a dip in the land lay a small pond. She'd gone fishing there every summer during her childhood.

A line of trees formed protection for a woodsy canyon that extended from the edge of the property inward. And obscured the view of the far-off ranch house and the big barn. Which was a blessing. In the winter, the hands and—most importantly—the foreman would stick close to the house and barn.

And if Ben Taylor saw her loitering near the family ranch, he'd likely throw her over his shoulder to get her onto the property. At least, that's what he'd threatened several times when he'd approached her in town.

But back here, there was no one to see her.

Maybe he wouldn't really haul her bodily onto the

property, but every time he'd accosted her—once in the grocery store—she'd felt raw for days.

He couldn't understand why she didn't run back to what had been her home for the first twelve years of her life.

Her dad was gone now, and Ben was her only link to the Circle A ranch. Since her dad's death two years ago, Ben had emailed her monthly reports. Long detailed descriptions of what was going on with the property and herd, along with information about maintenance the house had required.

Those reports hadn't brought back memories the way seeing the Circle A in person did.

She thought about starting the car. Following the dirt road almost another mile. Turning into the drive her father had had graveled and lined with a black plank fence—barbed wire was too cheap for her dad.

She couldn't do it.

She dialed her cell phone instead.

"What's up, Lila?" her friend Melody answered. "It's too cold to go skydiving. Or hot air ballooning. Or—"

"Build a snowman?" Lila teased.

"There's no snow. Only ice."

"Build an ice-man?"

Melody giggled. "What's going on?"

"Just checking on you. You all set for the day?" A part of her hoped Melody would decide to close her Main Street dress shop for the day so they could hang out. Maybe not skydiving, but Lila was a pro at devising fun. The freelance bookkeeping work that supplemented her income could be put off until later.

But Melody was opening the store today and Lila's fun would have to wait.

The coil in her chest eased as instead she started the car and pulled a three-point turn. She would take the long way back to the two-lane state highway, not daring to chance passing Ben's farm truck on her way.

Maybe coming to Redbud Trails had been a mistake.

It had been an impulse, like so many of the things she did. Probably a bad one, given that she hadn't planned well and had run out of gas a few miles out of town. If Melody Carter, a resident and now one of Lila's closest friends, hadn't stopped, Lila would have been forced to endure a humiliating hike to town to buy a gallon of gas.

Melody carried an extra gallon in her trunk, just in case. She must've been a Girl Scout in her childhood. When it was Melody's turn to schedule the weekly girls' night outing, she planned everything down to the last detail.

Like the night they'd binged on three Jane Austen movies in a row. Melody had timed their between-movie breaks to make sure they stayed on schedule.

She and Anna Brown, soon-to-be Anna Matthews, were Lila's two best friends.

She hadn't had friends in a long time. She hadn't let herself get close to anyone.

Maybe coming home had made her nostalgic, or maybe the constant loneliness, keeping everyone at arms'-length had worn her down.

If she wasn't going home, then she needed to get out of Redbud Trails. Cut ties.

First, she had to get through Christmas.

Somehow the elderly Mrs. Potts, a pillar of the local church since Lila had been a girl, had wrangled her in to being a part of the live nativity the small-town church would hold the three weeknights leading up to Christmas.

Lila hadn't been able to say no to the older woman when Mrs. Potts had caught her outside church last week.

She'd lost her touch.

She could only hope she wouldn't lose any more of herself before she could get out of town.

She slowed to a crawl before she reached the turn-off for the highway, and not because of ice on the road. He was still there. A neighbor.

The bay gelding she'd noticed on her last trip out here —and several times before—stood close to the rusty barbed wire fence. Lila could see the definition of his ribs. His mane and tail were matted and unkempt. Lila couldn't see any food in the small fenced pen. Nor was there any shelter for the animal. Had it weathered the ice storm out in the elements?

Lila blinked at the tears blurring her vision even as she reached for her cell phone.

She dialed the number by memory.

The man on the other end answered with a grunt. "What now, Lila?"

"Eric, he's starving."

The county sheriff sighed in her ear. "I've made two visits to the owner. He claims the animal is fine."

The animal. "He's *starving*," Lila repeated.

"There's a legal process," the sheriff said.

She tuned him out. She'd heard it before. He had the power to remove that horse, but his hands were tied.

It made her so *angry.*

She flexed her mittened hands on the steering wheel, knowing there was nothing she could do this very moment but hating that she had to drive away.

She was powerless.

CHAPTER 2

*B*en Taylor stood in the church vestibule and allowed the diminutive Velma Potts to drape a brown robe from the VBS costume closet over his shoulders.

It was weird being in the building with everything quiet and dark. He was used to all the lights on, not just the few in the foyer that Velma had lit. And the familiar smell of coffee and donuts was missing.

"I'm glad to see you're getting back in the spirit of the holiday, dear."

He tried to smile, but it felt more like his lips stretched across his teeth. He didn't feel in the spirit. Not at all.

Did they really expect him to stand outside on the lawn for hours in this getup?

He would freeze his butt off. Already he fought the urge to rub the scar under his ribs, just thinking about it tightening up in the cold.

Why had he agreed to this, again?

Because Velma had told him Lila had agreed. And he was ready to end this Mexican standoff they'd been playing at.

Although worrying about Lila provided some distraction from his memories of Mia. Christmas had always been Mia's favorite season. She'd decorate the entire house well before Thanksgiving and sing carols from Halloween through December twenty-fifth.

After her death four years ago, he'd boxed up the decorations and tried to ignore the season passing. Stayed on the ranch.

Sometimes he still walked in the door after a long day in the barn and expected to see her just around the corner.

Maybe he should've moved away after her death. Maybe that would've been easier. They'd fallen in love here in Redbud Trails. Made memories that he relived everywhere he went.

But he'd made Tom Andrews, Lila's father, a promise before the old man had died. To bring Lila home and teach her the ranch. Turn it over to her when she was ready.

It was a difficult task when she refused to set foot on the property. And when he saw the shadows in her eyes every time he mentioned it.

He didn't understand why she wouldn't come home. She was the rightful owner of a nice-sized ranch. A profitable one.

But she hadn't come home even when her parents had

died. She cashed the checks he sent to her ever-changing address. Never answered his emails, including the last one that he'd intended to push her buttons. He'd asked if she wanted to sell the place.

Was she or was she not going to take over the operation?

He was determined to find out, and if he had to wear this costume and freeze his bum off for a couple of days, so be it.

Lila came in the door with a rush of cold air, her hair blowing out of her bun and into her eyes.

She brushed at the fine wisps, her head turning toward him and Velma.

And when her hair and her hand had cleared her vision, her gaze collided with his.

"What...?" Her eyes snagged on the robe or his chest—he'd like to think it was his chest—and stuck.

"Am I doing here?" He finished when it seemed she wouldn't complete her sentence. "Getting fitted, same as you."

She started backing away, shaking her head, but good ol' Velma was too quick for her. Velma had Lila's elbow in her clutches before Lila'd even realized it. She pushed the shocked woman almost shoulder-to-shoulder with him and draped some tan material around her.

"I don't think this is a good idea," Lila mumbled.

He was starting to agree with her as their shoulders brushed and a *twang* of something lit up his insides. Looking sideways at her, he couldn't help noticing the wind outside had pinked her cheeks. Usually she kept her hair more tamed, pulled back in a severe braid or pony-tail, but her bun was slipping, and strands of her dark, almost black hair curled around her face.

Her dishevelment made her seem more approachable. And he knew she wasn't. She was as cool as this frigid winter.

It wasn't the first time he'd felt the *zing* of attraction between them. He really couldn't help it—Lila was slender and tall and exceptionally beautiful. He was six foot himself, and even now her forehead was about even with his chin.

The perfect height to kiss.

The thought struck him right between the eyebrows. Painfully, he shook off his distraction.

"I think we can say this fits," he told Velma as he shrugged out of the costume. He draped it across a nearby high-backed chair then turned and crossed his arms, waiting for Lila to be finished.

He'd gotten this close to her. It was time to press her for a decision. Time for her to come home.

LILA SMELLED A SETUP. Either Ben had been behind Mrs. Potts wrangling her into playing Mary, or he'd watched her get wrangled and then had volunteered.

She stood numbly as Mrs. Potts draped a robe over her shoulders, then clucked when Lila was apparently too tall for the women's robe.

"I'll have to alter this one." Mrs. Potts tucked her into a pale blue robe that fell past her ankles but was voluminous up top. The older woman rifled through a small tin of sewing pins and started tucking in and pinning the excess fabric.

Sure, it was only three nights. And they were really supposed to stand next to each other silently—just present a visual of the nativity as it might've been all those centuries ago and allow whoever stopped by to interpret the beauty of the scene for themselves. They didn't even have to talk.

But since he'd worked for her dad and was a part of the ranch now, being around Ben made her feel things she'd rather forget about.

Hence the long hiatus from home.

She'd stuck her phone in her jeans' pocket before coming inside, and now it buzzed, startling her.

She jumped, and Mrs. Potts jumped, and as a result, Lila got pricked in the arm with a straight pin.

"Ow!"

"Dear, you've got to hold still."

Yeah, she'd had problems doing that her whole life.

"I'm really sorry. I need to take this phone call." And find a way to slip out a back door or something. They could find someone else to play Mary. Maybe Melody or Anna, either of whom was more suited to it than she was.

Mrs. Potts narrowed her eyes, taking the pins she'd been holding between her lips out. "I'm only half-done, dearie. You can't take the costume off yet, or we'll have to start all over."

"Fine." Her phone stopped buzzing against her leg, but

she turned and escaped down the hallway adjacent to the darkened sanctuary and slipped into the first classroom.

She didn't bother turning on the light. This was one of the kiddie classrooms, and seeing the art stapled to the walls would just bring back more painful memories she didn't need right now.

It smelled the same as it had fifteen years ago. Like pencil shavings and old linoleum.

She dug for her phone, and the screen lit up as she lifted it from her pocket.

Sheriff Eric.

"Did something change?" she asked. "Are you going to confiscate him?"

"Hello to you, too," the sheriff all but barked. He was her age, but she would swear he acted like a crotchety grandpa.

"Are you?"

He sighed. "I wish I had better news for you about the horse close to your place."

She bit back a correction that it wasn't *really* her place.

"Then what do you want?"

"You made all kinds of promises trying to get me to rescue that horse. Like that you'd take care of it. Put it somewhere nice and pay vet bills and feed it right."

"Yes, I did." Even though half of what she'd said had been stretching the truth. She'd been living in a tiny apartment since she returned to Redbud Trails. But surely Anna would give her space in her barn. And she had some money socked away from the penance funds her father had sent her. And a little saved from the free-lance bookkeeping jobs she picked up.

"I need to know if that offer is still good. I've got a mare the county just confiscated in about the same condition as the horse you described, and I need somewhere to put her."

Was this a ploy to try and get her to forget about the gelding? Because if it was, it wouldn't work.

But she also couldn't stand the thought of another animal being mistreated so badly.

"I'll take her," she blurted. She just didn't know *where* she'd take her.

He rattled off an address outside of town on the opposite side of where the Circle A was located and then said, "Be there in an hour. With a horse trailer."

He hung up, leaving her stunned and panicky. She'd thought he would deliver the horse to her. At least give her some time to get things set up. She didn't have a horse trailer. And where was she going to put the animal?

Mind whirling, she chewed on her lip.

Her impulsiveness had gotten her into scrapes before. And just like always, she would find a way to fix things.

It was what she did.

She dialed Anna and pressed the phone to her ear. Glanced toward the hallway, where a shadow shifted.

Velma coming after her? Or Ben?

Anna's voicemail message kicked on. Great.

"Hey, Anna! I need to see if you've got an empty stall where I can board a horse for...a little while. Also, can I borrow your horse trailer? Um...and your truck? I know it's a lot to ask but I promise I'll be really careful. And...it's sort of an emergency. Call me back, okay?"

Her stomach cramped. If she couldn't reach Anna soon, where could she find help?

Except for Anna and Melody, she'd been careful to avoid entanglements.

Then she straightened her shoulders. She would find a way. A horse depended on her now.

BEN SHIFTED his boots from where he eavesdropped outside the preschool classroom like a kiddie spying on his parents.

Lila spoke softly into her phone. Now it sounded like she'd called a rental car place in Weatherford. She questioned someone about whether they rented horse trailers.

Where was she getting a horse? She had ten at her disposal on the ranch. And an ATV.

He heard her frustrated sigh before the door that had been half-closed swung open. She almost walked into him, giving him a whiff of spicy-smelling shampoo.

She wobbled, and he reached out to steady her, but she was quick to shift out of his reach.

"What are you doing out here?" she demanded. "Spying on me?"

"Velma sent me after you. She needs to finish up."

She opened her mouth as if she would argue with

him, but then she shook her head slightly and pushed past him.

He trailed her down the hall and back into the foyer, where Velma was waiting with her pins.

"There you are, dear. I thought I'd lost you."

"Here I am. Unfortunately, I need to go." Lila didn't look at him.

"Oh no. I need to finish pinning this robe. We've only got a few days to get the costumes just right."

He could see Lila was upset, but she submitted to Velma's measuring and pinning, staring straight ahead, though the rapid movements of her eyes told him her mind was working.

She still pretended he wasn't here.

Lila might want to ignore him, but that didn't mean he had to take it.

"If you need help, why didn't you ask me?"

Now her eyes flicked to his. She returned her gaze to the obviously fascinating blank wall in front of her. "I don't need help."

And what he heard was *I don't need* your *help*.

"What's going on, dear?" Velma asked through her mouth full of pins. "You all right?"

"*Yes*." Lila glared at him. "I'm working on a...project. And I think I've got it handled. I'm just waiting on Anna to call me back."

He crossed his arms again, staring at her as she stared back. She was so stubborn.

But he wasn't letting this chance pass him by.

Lila's relief at shaking Ben was short-lived. She found him leaning against the drivers' side door of her Chevelle, the collar of his fleece-lined jean jacket pulled up. His arms were still crossed. It seemed like his constant disapproval seeped out through his stance whenever he looked at her.

"Let's make a deal," he said. "I'll help you out tonight if you come out to the ranch."

Anna still hadn't returned her call. She'd tried twice more, even texted Anna's fiancé Kelly, but no one had returned her messages.

It irritated her that Ben had eavesdropped on her phone calls, but in the last half hour, her situation had gone from difficult to desperate. If she could convince Eric that she could care for this horse, maybe she could spur him on to help the gelding.

"You need a horse trailer. I've got a trailer."

She didn't want to take his deal, but time was short, and it looked like she had no choice.

"Fine."

Even with the dimness of twilight, she didn't miss the flare of triumph in his eyes.

It sparked something in her. Attraction maybe? No, certainly not. "I'm in a hurry. Can I have your keys?"

His lips widened in a slow, wicked smile. "I never said I was giving you the truck. I'll take you where you need to go."

CHAPTER 3

The mare was pregnant. And underweight. Her hooves and teeth were in horrid condition.

After a half hour car ride—where Lila had mulishly given him the silent treatment—they'd arrived at a small farm he wasn't familiar with. Half of the barbed wire fencing that separated the property from the road was knocked down. The mobile home was badly in need of a paint job, maybe a new roof.

And then, that horse. It curdled Ben's stomach to see it.

The sheriff argued with the property owner near the mobile home a good fifty yards from the open-air corral where Ben and Lila stood beside the trailer he'd backed up to the gate. She had her elbows clasped in her hands, like her coat wasn't doing its job. His wasn't either, the cold night air creeping beneath his coat to tighten up his scar tissue. He breathed through it.

Every time the occasional shout punctuated the chill, Lila's head jerked in that direction.

He'd thought she was *buying* a horse. When he'd discovered she was helping rescue this one, he'd been shocked.

The fact that she was so obviously frightened by the property owner's anger but sticking through her fear with that stubborn tilt of her chin was also something he didn't want to think too hard about.

All they needed was to get the animal loaded up, but the mare paced nervously by the fence on the opposite side of the corral.

Lila slowly circled the corral, heading away from the trailer. Several yards down the fence, she propped her elbows on the top railing. What was she doing? Watching the horse? He couldn't read her face, though he wanted to.

Ben glanced back at the sheriff, who gave a thumbs up above his head, now talking more quietly with the homeowner.

Ben took a bucket of oats from a hook in the back of the trailer and stepped just inside the pen. He rattled the bucket.

The mare's ears flicked forward, but she took another loop in her anxious pacing.

The sheriff joined them and with a nod to Ben, moved around behind the pen. He gave the animal some encouragement—Ben was too far away to hear his words —but she only shied into the center of the pen, now well away from all three of them.

Someone was going to have to go inside and get her.

Lila passed him—when had she left the railing?—a long coil of rope in her hands.

"Lila," he hissed.

Of course she ignored him. Stubborn woman. She meandered toward the horse, taking her time, slowly looping the rope in what he recognized as a temporary halter. If she could get close enough to slip it over the animal's head, maybe they could lead her into the trailer.

But if she got too close and the horse spooked, she could get knocked down or trampled.

Instinct held him back as she approached the animal, still at a snail's pace. He didn't want to be the one to scare the animal.

Her back to him, Lila spoke softly. She was nearly there.

Then, before she'd reached the animal, she stopped short.

His heart pounded. Had she seen something, some twitch of an ear or flare of a nostril that he hadn't? Was she in danger?

Balanced on the balls of his feet, he still hesitated.

Everything seemed frozen in the cold. Everything except the white clouds bursting from the horse's nostrils.

As he watched, the horse took one tentative step in Lila's direction. Then another.

He held his breath. Lila raised her hand and touched the bridge of the animal's nose, slowly rubbed up to its forelock. She raised the rope, allowed the horse to sniff it, then slipped the halter over the horse's head.

She didn't even have to give a tug. As she turned toward him, the animal came even with her and walked beside her across the pen.

It balked once, with a bob of its head, when they neared Ben. To his extreme surprise, Lila reached out and laid her palm on his forearm.

The animal blew out a breath and then seemed to accept Lila's gesture.

Ben was blown away by the sight of tears rolling unchecked down Lila's face.

He stood still as she led the animal into the trailer and secured it. She still murmured to the animal, a continuous stream of words. Giving comfort, but who would comfort her?

What had made her cry?

Since she'd returned to town, he'd seen a cool, stubborn woman always in control, even when she was acting impulsive and adventurous.

But not tonight.

When she exited the trailer, her eyes glittered in the starlight, but her face was dry.

"Are you all right?" It was a dumb question considering what he'd just seen, but he was a simple cowboy and what could he say? A woman's tears still tripped him up, even after the five years of marriage he'd shared with Mia.

"I'm fine." The coolness had returned to her voice, and her chin jutted out stubbornly.

He made sure the animal was secure, then closed the trailer doors as she spoke to the sheriff and climbed into his truck. He got in and cranked the heat up, shucking his leather gloves and flexing his fingers against the cold that had settled into them. The ache in his chest would take longer to fade. He blew on his fingers, watching her from the corner of his eye.

Her shoulders were straight, her head high, and she stared out the window as if he weren't there.

Big surprise.

Unfortunately, he couldn't unsee what he'd seen tonight.

Lila had more layers than he—or maybe anyone— knew about. And who did she have in her life to dig into those layers and make sure she was all right? Her family was gone, and although he knew she'd made close friends with Anna and Melody since she'd come to town, he also had seen how well she could pretend that everything was all right.

Suddenly, Lila seemed way too much like the battered mare riding in the trailer behind them. But who would rescue her?

LILA KNEW the silence couldn't last as Ben carefully navigated the rutted back roads, aiming the truck back toward Redbud Trails.

She hadn't meant for him to see her tears.

Obviously, this was one of those times that her impulsivity was going to bite her in the butt.

She hadn't been back on a horse since her childhood. She'd been thrown from the horse of life and thrown good. Running had been her M.O. and it had served her well. Until now.

Was she having a quarter-life crisis? She'd read a news article about the phenomenon happening to kids who graduated college and then didn't know what to do with themselves.

A crisis was the only thing that could've led her back to Redbud Trails.

She hadn't thought about the repercussions of getting involved when she'd called the sheriff about that mistreated horse near the Circle A. And when he'd offered her a part in helping *this* horse, she hadn't refused.

Had she somehow thought she would be able to rescue this animal from afar, without getting close enough to touch?

Her heart had broken when she'd seen the neglected animal. Of course, that broken heart hadn't been enough to get her inside that pen. No, she'd had no intention of approaching it until she'd seen the whites of the mare's eyes, her intense fear of the men.

Lila hadn't really thought about her actions. A purely impulsive move.

She certainly hadn't realized her heart would break all over again just by touching the horse, by getting close enough to make that connection, small as it was.

"You wanna grab something to eat? The diner's still open."

Ben's words startled her out of the tenuous quiet she'd slipped into, her eyes on the fields passing them by.

"I'm okay."

She just wanted to get away from him. Get back to her apartment and lick her wounds.

"You should eat. It's gonna be a long night. Vet's on her way, but it might be awhile until we can get this gal settled."

We? There was no *we* here.

And then she realized he hadn't taken the turn to Anna's ranch. "I thought you were taking me to Anna's place."

"You thought wrong. You've been away from home long enough. It's time, don't you think?"

Frustration rose in a flood, and tears pricked her eyes. Which made her even more angry. "I know you worked for my dad. Was this some kind of last wish he laid on you? To get me home no matter how much I don't want to be there?"

"There must be a part of you that wants to be there, or you wouldn't come sit up on that hill so often. Your car could probably drive out there on its own by now."

His calm, even words struck home, and she felt the familiar tightness take over her chest, making it hard to breathe. She'd thought she'd been so sneaky, driving the back way and staying well away from the farm buildings.

She turned her head to stare blindly out the window. She'd promised Eric she would take care of the mare. And if Ben already had the vet on the way out to the family ranch, that was that, wasn't it?

But it also meant she would be trapped there without a ride, because she'd allowed Ben to drive from the church parking lot.

Once again, she cursed her impulsivity.

"My wife was estranged from her family." He offered the words conversationally.

She was curious enough to turn her head. "You're married?"

He chuckled dryly. "Don't sound so surprised. I've got a steady job. I've been told I'm not bad to look at."

"You're humble," she said when she really meant the opposite.

"Mia used to say the same thing."

And then his use of past tense registered.

"She died four years ago this Christmas," he said as if he'd sensed her exact thoughts.

"I'm sorry." The words were inadequate and she knew it. Hadn't she heard them plenty herself? They didn't change the stinging loss, the aching emptiness inside.

He shifted in his seat. "She reconciled with her parents just before she passed. It was one of the most important things to her, there at the end."

He was preaching at her. As if he knew one iota of what she'd been through, what she'd done. "I wasn't estranged from my dad."

"Just from his life here."

By dad's choice. He was the one who'd sent her away.

He'd come to visit her where she'd happened to land each year. They'd pretended that the ranch didn't exist, and she'd been happy not to talk about those painful things.

There was no way she could share that pain with Ben. He might understand her loss, but he wouldn't—couldn't —understand her guilt.

She changed the subject. "What was she like? Your wife?"

"She was pretty"—he glanced at her briefly—"like you. She was a blonde, though."

Her cheeks flushed at his words. Ben found her pretty? Not that it mattered. He was too entrenched in her parents' ranch. Nothing could be between them, no matter how attractive she found him.

CHAPTER 4

*B*ack at the Circle A, Ben helped Lila unload the mare into a large box stall, mostly unused, in the back corner of the stable. It was usually used for mares when they gave birth, so it seemed the best choice now. Well away from the other animals, if there was any disease she needed to be quarantined for, she should be safe back here.

After visiting the rundown little farm and knowing that Lila hadn't been back in years, he saw the place how she must see it. Barn clean and airy, smelling of fresh hay. Warm and out of the cutting wind.

He couldn't help but notice Lila's tension, though she was kind to Sarah, the veterinarian, whom the sheriff had called for them.

From the moment his tires had crunched onto the front drive for the quarter-mile trek to the compound, she'd been silent and tense.

Her arms came around her midsection once, when

the big house had come into sight, as if she were holding herself together. Somehow she looked smaller, seemed to shrink inside herself. This was not the Lila who'd never been afraid to tell him to go to heck.

There was a small part of him that wanted to reach for her. Comfort her, somehow.

It was like seeing her tears when they'd picked up the neglected horse had pulled back the curtain. He would never see her the same way again.

But when she caught him looking, she straightened, shifted into a loose-limbed, confidence-exuding stance.

He knew better. She was hiding what she really felt behind a mask.

He was the one who'd brought her here. He'd done it to bring resolution—the ranch needed an owner, not just a caretaker.

But bringing her here hurt her, somehow. And he'd done it, so it was his job to fix it.

BEN WAS DRIVING HER CRAZY. Hovering like a mother hen, except when the vet asked him questions.

It irked her that the vet assumed he knew more about the horse than she did. They both had the same information, but the horse had been turned over into her care, not his.

Being here was difficult.

Perhaps she could hitch a ride home with the vet, who was almost done with her exam. Lila hadn't been acquainted with the leggy blonde before tonight, but she liked the woman's no-nonsense approach.

But if she ran off, Lila had a feeling Ben would come after her and demand that she fulfill her side of their bargain. He was determined like that.

Hadn't she thought earlier today that maybe it was time to wrap things up and leave Redbud Trails behind?

Maybe she could just Band-Aid it. Get this visit over with. Go through with the nativity. Be packed by Christmas morning.

The vet wrapped up with the portable ultrasound machine and met them outside the stall while the technician packed their things into the truck.

"Her colt is due any day."

"Can she—is she in any condition to go through labor?" Lila asked.

The vet glanced at Ben, and Lila's gaze followed.

His expression had closed off. His face had gone white. Something in Lila's question or Sarah's non-answer had unnerved him. But surely they'd had plenty of cattle born each spring. This couldn't be much different.

"I don't know," Sarah said. "If we can get some nutrients into her, fatten her up a little before the big event, it will help. If she starts having trouble, call me."

She gave them both further instructions on feeding the mare and some pain meds she gave them for her teeth after the extensive filing she'd been given, but Lila found it hard to pay attention. Her gaze kept wandering out the barn doors to the ranch house.

Finally, the vet drove off. Which left the two of them and the unnatural tension.

"You want to go up to the main house?" Ben asked.

She really didn't. She blinked against those last, vivid memories.

He seemed to realize she couldn't without her saying so. He took her elbow and turned her toward the small cottage that created a triangle with the barn and house. "I bet Norma"—the housekeeper—"left some supper for me. Since you wouldn't let me stop at the diner, I'll bring it over to my place. It'll be unlocked. Why don't you go in, make yourself comfortable."

She walked across the yard on wooden legs, not minding the cold wind as it slapped at her cheeks. She paused on the threshold, but a burst of wind at her back pressed her forward, and she found herself inside before she'd really thought it through.

She'd been in the foreman's house maybe once during her childhood. With free run of the big house and the barn, she'd had no need to visit before.

She flipped on the switch next to the door. Lights flicked on, a lamp in two corners of the room and a can light above a rock fireplace.

If she'd expected a bachelor pad, she'd have been sorely disappointed. It was cute. Trendy, even. A pair of warm, neutral couches with brightly colored pillows flanked the fireplace on both sides and invited her to sit. A squat butcher-block coffee table was covered in several farming magazines and a pad of lined paper.

Interesting. No Christmas decor. Not one Christmas card on the coffee table. Not one stocking or poinsettia.

Several pictures lined the mantel above the fireplace and without conscious effort, her feet had taken her closer.

Ben and a pretty blonde woman in their wedding finery. In contrast to the frown lines he constantly wore when he looked at Lila, his smile was easy and light. And his bride was beautiful.

There was also a picture of Ben in his late teens sporting a broad belt buckle and holding what must've been a prize-winning saddle. An older man—his dad?—had an arm slung over Ben's shoulder. He'd competed and won in some long-ago rodeo.

Pushed halfway behind the rodeo photograph, as if someone had put it out of sight on purpose, was another photograph.

With a guilty look at the front door behind her, she reached out and pulled the framed photo out, just enough that she could see it.

It was a black and white ultrasound. She tilted her head to one side and the other, trying to see... was that a tiny foot? Was this an unborn baby? *Ben's* unborn baby?

She looked toward the room beyond this living area. A kitchen, darkened because she hadn't gone further and turned on the light. Was there a child back there somewhere? Asleep?

Or had Ben sent his child away?

She couldn't imagine someone as responsible as he

not supporting his flesh and blood, no matter the personal cost.

The mystery made her cold. And nervous.

She tugged her coat closer. Caught sight of the TV remote buried underneath one of the magazines on the table. She fumbled it in her hurry to pick it up but managed to turn on the TV mounted to the wall opposite the fireplace.

The noise helped.

Until the cowboy came in the door with a burst of cold air.

SOMETHING HAD SPOOKED Lila in the few minutes he'd been at the main house to retrieve the pan of lasagna the housekeeper had left for him. Norma's duties didn't include cooking for him, but she'd done it anyway since Mia had died.

It was late for supper, and he was starving, so he ignored his fidgeting houseguest—who hadn't even taken her coat off—and the blaring TV for the moment and went into the kitchen, flipping on the light as he went.

The glare off the yellowing linoleum momentarily blinded him, as usual. Mia had campaigned their entire married life to redo the flooring throughout the cottage. They'd scraped and saved until they could afford it, and then Mia had been hospitalized, and it had been too late.

He should replace it. But he just squinted against the glare and set the foil-wrapped lasagna pan and a thick binder he'd grabbed from Tom's office on the counter.

She followed him, leaned one shoulder against the doorjamb. He nodded to the TV visible behind her. "I'm not really into Christmas movies." Mia had been.

She glanced around in an exaggerated manner. "You don't seem to be into the holiday at all. Even I have a tiny tree in my apartment."

He turned his back and grabbed two plates from the upper cabinet next to the sink. Thinking about Christmas just hurt too much.

When Mia died, he'd been forced to come home and take down her boxes of decorations. He'd shoved them in the back of the attic, and there they'd stayed ever since.

If that made him a Scrooge, then...so be it.

"You'll shoot your eye out, kid."

"Hmm?" He glanced over his shoulder, but she'd turned so that her back was to the door and her gaze was on the Christmas movie. He'd hoped she'd turn it off.

And then the kid got shoved down the slide at Santa's village, and Ben found himself smiling. Even chuckling, just a little.

Lila glanced over her shoulder, their smiles and gazes connecting.

She averted her eyes quickly.

"You don't look very comfortable," he said as he spooned out two healthy portions of the lasagna onto the plates.

Her eyebrows crunched together.

"I told you to come inside and make yourself comfortable," he reminded her.

She looked down at herself. She was still wearing her coat, though her scarf was open at the neck.

She shrugged. "I guess I was hoping we weren't staying long."

He gave her a mock glare. "Long enough to talk about what needs talking about."

But she distracted him by quoting the movie again as she shed her coat and laid it across the back of the couch. She came into the kitchen and located the cutlery drawer.

Their shoulders bumped in the close space as she stepped past him to set the small nook table where he and Mia had eaten so many meals together.

He got hung up with both plates of steaming lasagna in hand, staring at those place settings.

Lila was the first woman who'd come in here since Mia's death, and looking at the silverware set out at exact angles to the table's edge made him intensely aware of it.

He cleared away the frog of emotion in his throat. "Why don't we eat on the sofa?"

She took one of the plates of steaming food from him as he scooped up the cutlery from the table.

Sitting across from her on the sofas was better—he and Mia had always sat side-by-side, sometimes snuggling under an old quilt together. The distance and being face-to-face with Lila helped him separate things in his mind.

It didn't stop his awareness of her dancing eyes.

The movie cut to a commercial, a familiar jingle that

had played countless times each Christmas season that he could remember.

And Lila was suddenly singing along.

She looked at him, raising her brows, daring him to join her.

No way. He shoved a bite of lasagna in his mouth.

But he still found himself humming along by the end.

He didn't mean to let down his guard, but by the time the movie was over, they'd debated pros and cons of fictional Christmas gifts, they'd laughed themselves silly when the Christmas meal got eaten by hound dogs, and she'd even made them both bowls of popcorn and mugs of hot chocolate—the real thing, not the powder mix from a packet.

He opened his mouth to bring up the ranch and her plans, but something hit his cheek and dropped to his lap.

Incredulous, he looked down on the kernel of popcorn resting on his jeans pocket.

"What was that?" he asked. He looked up into her dancing eyes and got totally distracted.

And another kernel flew across the space between them and hit his nose.

He raised his brows. "Have we gone back to junior high? Really?"

Her lashes lowered, covering those expressive eyes. It gave him just enough time to scoop up a handful of corn from his bowl and launch it at her. It showered over her and she squealed.

And retaliated.

Five minutes later, his living room was covered in popcorn and he was breathless from laughing so hard.

"Uncle!" He raised both hands in surrender.

She watched him with narrowed eyes. Maybe making sure he wasn't going to launch another attack on her, but finally she relaxed enough to sit back on the couch.

The credits changed on the TV and her eyes cut there. "Oh, I love this one."

Another Christmas movie. One that had been Mia's favorite. This time the stab of pain didn't burn quite so badly. Maybe dulled by the laughter he'd just shared with Lila.

When was the last time he'd laughed like that? Allowed himself to fall into someone's eyes, even from across the room?

He hadn't.

Being with her like this, with her legs curled beneath her and her walls down, felt like being with a friend.

And he realized the warmth and laughter Lila brought with her had been sorely missing in his life since Mia's death.

He still needed to talk with her about her long-term plans for the ranch. And he had to drive her home, but he'd been awake since before dawn, and he found himself drifting off with his head against the back of the couch.

He woke disoriented in the middle of the night with a crick in his neck as a pair of headlights swept the wall opposite. Someone had turned around in the drive.

He got up, rubbing one hand over his gritty eyes.

Lila was gone.

He stumbled into the kitchen to find their plates rinsed and stacked in the bottom of the sink, the silverware lined up neatly on top. Their hot chocolate mugs had also been washed and were lined up next to the sink with their handles at exactly the same angle.

It seemed kind of OCD for someone as impulsive as Lila was.

The binder of financial information was gone. In its place was a small origami Christmas tree, standing upright.

CHAPTER 5

"Spill it, girl."

Lila finished her massive yawn and sunk down lower into the vinyl booth at the local diner.

Remembering how Anna had tried to ignore both her and Melody when they'd been hot on the trail of juicy details when she'd been falling for Kelly, Lila had little hope that the avoidance tactic would work.

"You didn't start without me, did you?" Anna blew her hair out of her face and shoved in next to Lila, even though there was a perfectly good seat on the side of the booth next to Melody.

"She's pretty clammed up, especially for someone who needed a ride in the middle of the night."

"It was eleven. Not the middle of the night."

Melody chuckled. "Felt like it. I was up at five doing inventory for the shop."

A flare of guilt pinged in Lila's gut. She hadn't meant to stay so long at the Circle A last night.

She hadn't meant to make friends with Ben, either. She'd meant to distract him from talking about the ranch and had begun goofing off in response to the movie on the television, but then their talk had turned to Christmases past—though they both carefully tiptoed around the issue of his wife's death—and she'd found him funny and engaging. Even when he'd become adorably drowsy and nodded off, she'd felt something inside opening up to him. It had been a long time since she'd spent time with any man without that spring inside her coiling tight.

She was starting to like him.

And that was dangerous.

She had to remember that he wanted something from her, something she wasn't sure she could give. A decision. His last email had said she needed to fish or cut bait. Okay, not those terms exactly, but he'd definitely pushed her.

A waitress set a cup of coffee in front of Anna, who thanked her with a nod, then refocused her attention on Lila. "So...?"

"So...nothing. We rescued a horse—a pregnant mare—and he fed me dinner at his place."

Anna raised her coffee cup to her mouth, and her engagement ring flashed in the morning sunlight streaming through the windows.

Lila's stomach pitched, and she shoved her half-full cup toward the center of the table. The visible reminder of Anna's upcoming nuptials spun the coil inside her, knowing that she was going to disappoint her friends. They didn't seem to notice.

"There's something more going on," Melody guessed. She leaned over the table, eyes alight with interest. Her hair had a bright green streak in it today. "You've been avoiding the man since you came back to town."

"Because he runs my dad's ranch."

Melody shook her head slightly. "That's not why you're jumpy when he comes around."

"I'm not jumpy."

Anna and Melody shared a glance. "She's attracted to him," Melody said.

She'd never admit to it. But apparently she didn't have to. Her friends had noticed all on their own, and they wouldn't listen even if she tried to deny it. Still...

"He's overbearing," she said.

"He's cute," Anna countered.

He wasn't. He was virile. Rugged. Masculine.

But if she protested Anna's description, they would never let her forget it.

"He's still grieving," Lila said.

Anna and Melody's crazy interest dimmed. Slightly. Anna ran her index finger around the edge of her cup. "You can't grieve forever," she said softly. "Maybe he's ready to move on."

She'd seen the way he'd reacted when she'd set the table, how he'd rerouted them to the living room. The foreman's house had his wife's stamp all over it, and Ben hadn't changed a thing. Not that she blamed him.

"He's tied to this town, and I'm not," she said.

Now Melody looked dumbstruck, though Anna's expression revealed no surprise.

"You're leaving?" Melody blurted.

She hadn't made up her mind, but since when did that stop her? She was Miss Impulsive, right?

"After Christmas."

Melody shook her head. Her mouth opened and closed, but no sound came out.

The coil in Lila's chest wound tighter. She didn't want to hurt these ladies, her friends, either. She hadn't tried very hard to rebuff them when Melody had included her in their group those first few days she'd been back in town.

"You've stayed this long," Anna said, voice quiet and grave. "We'd kind of hoped you'd decide to stay for good."

She didn't do forevers. Didn't deserve them.

"What about the wedding?" Anna asked.

That's right. Her friend had asked her to be a bridesmaid in her Valentine's Day wedding. Lila had put off giving an answer.

"You could come back," Melody whispered, her voice shrinking with the gravity of the situation.

But Lila shook her head slightly.

"Was it so bad, being back on the ranch?" Melody asked.

She kept her eyes on her coffee cup. Cold now. "I couldn't even go inside the big house."

Even though she wasn't looking, she caught Melody's crinkled brows and the questioning look she sent Anna across the table.

"Can I tell her?" Anna asked.

Lila shrugged. "It's public knowledge." But that didn't stop her voice from cracking over the words.

"I was almost fourteen, so that would've made you...what, twelve?"

Lila didn't answer. Couldn't.

"Lila lost her best friend."

The words were simple. They didn't tell the real story. Lila's fault.

Those moments, frozen in time in her memories, started playing in a loop. Too bright. Too much.

Tears stung the back of her throat. "I need to go."

But Anna didn't budge. Instead, she laid her hand over Lila's on the seat cushion. "It's okay to let us in."

But it wasn't.

The counselor at the boarding school her father had sent her to made her sit through several sessions of grief counseling. After her third college boyfriend had broken up with her and called her an ice queen, she'd sought counseling on her own.

It hadn't helped. Only left her with more questions about herself.

Maybe they were right. Maybe something had broken in her when Andrea had died. Maybe she couldn't connect.

But then... every time she was in Ben's presence, she felt too connected. Overwhelmed from the inside out.

IT's *okay to let us in.*

Thirty-some odd hours later, Lila couldn't get her

friends' words out of her head. An afternoon snow squall had come and gone. Dinnertime was near.

She found herself in the sanctuary of the little Redbud Trails church, searching for wisdom. Huddled on one of the pews with her head bent on her clasped hands, she sent up prayer after prayer.

But just like most times since the accident, she received no tangible answer.

Was she supposed to stay? Or go?

She got up to leave.

Where the foyer had been dark and quiet when she'd come inside earlier, now the lights were on and a crowd bustled through, greeting each other.

What was going on?

"You stalking me, cowgirl?"

She whirled around at Ben's voice. The cowboy was shedding his coat and hat near the outer doors.

"I was..." She motioned inanely to the sanctuary, but someone had called out a greeting to him, and he'd nodded his head, distracted. "What's going on?" she asked when his gaze returned to her.

"It's youth night. C'mon."

Before she could protest, he'd taken her hand and swept her up in the jostling group making their way down the hall to the kitchen. The door to the multi-purpose room beyond it was open and bright, and chattering voices spilled out.

Youth night?

Ben dragged her into the long commercial kitchen, where a couple of other people were unloading groceries from several brown bags onto a counter. Someone had thrown open the garage-style doors that led to the multipurpose room beyond. It was crawling with teenagers.

"Hey, man. Ashley." Ben exchanged a fist bump with another handsome cowboy and threw a nod at the woman behind him.

The woman had been half-hidden behind the broad cowboy, but when she turned to greet them, Lila took in her proud bearing—military?—and the fact that she only had use of her left arm.

"I'm Ashley Michaels," she said to Lila with a smile. "This is my husband, Ryan."

Gold rings flashed in the bright kitchen lights as they both waved a little.

Lila nodded a greeting but didn't engage the woman in conversation. She would've slipped right back out the door—she didn't have time for this—except for Ben's hand warm at her lower back.

Somehow she found herself stationed between Ben and Ashley at a prep counter, wielding a chopping knife with a pile of tomatoes growing by the second as Ben washed them in the sink. Apparently they were making a mountain of tacos.

Ashley wielded a knife of her own, chopping heads of lettuce with a skill that belied her handicap.

"You don't seem to have any trouble," Lila said, a little admiration in her voice.

"Just don't offer to open her jars," Ryan said.

Ashley tossed an aggravated look over her shoulder, but Ryan just winked.

Obviously Lila was missing some kind of inside joke.

"How did you get involved in youth night?" she asked Ben.

"These two lassoed me into it."

Shouts heralded a new group of arrivals in the giant room.

Lila's head came up, and she caught sight of a couple of teen girls with features so alike they must have been twins, though their hair and clothes were opposite—one wore jeans, a football jersey and tennis shoes, while the other wore a plaid skirt, a sweater, and leather boots. Behind them—with them?—was Weston Moore. Lila wasn't acquainted with him, but she couldn't help remembering how Melody had been drawn to him last fall. As far as she knew, Melody had never done anything about her interest.

Weston rounded up several young men, and they began unfolding long tables from where they'd been folded up against the wall. She imagined they would drag out the old aluminum chairs next.

"Heard you've got a foaling mare on your hands," Ashley said.

Lila flicked a glance at Ben, but he'd turned his back to grab something from the counter opposite.

"Ryan and I manage the feed store," Ashley said.

Lila nodded. Was that the local gossip hub or something?

A piercing bark sounded from the multi-purpose room, and Lila's head came up again. A huge German Shepherd Dog across the room stood watching the three boys who dribbled the basketball between tables and around chairs.

Ashley whistled three notes, and the dog sat on his haunches. That was some obedience.

"Want me to go check on him?" Ryan asked.

But Ashley shook her head. "He just got excited about the ball."

The dog panted and stared at the ball with intense focus. With his ears cocked forward, she could see that one of his ears was just a stub. Had he and Ashley been in combat and been wounded?

"That's your dog?"

"Yeah." Ashley shook her head slightly, a smile playing around the corners of her mouth. "He's a little obsessed with balls. He's not allowed in the kitchen, or I'd have him lie down in here."

"A *little obsessed*?" Ryan echoed, a disbelieving tone audible even over the meat frying in the huge skillet in front of him.

Ashley shook her head again. "Ryan got knocked over once throwing the tennis ball for Atlas."

"He almost took my arm off."

"Well, I told you not to do that silly dance. Holding it up over your head was an invitation." Regardless of Ryan's teasing, the dog was incredibly well-trained not to chase after the kids. He stayed put.

Lila found herself smiling at the young couple's bickering. It was obvious from the scorching glances they kept sending each other that they loved each other.

Ben responded to Ryan's ribbing with an awful joke

and the three of them laughed. He belonged. Ryan and Ashley belonged.

But she didn't. Not really.

BEN DIDN'T KNOW why Lila had been at the church, but he'd seen his chance and grabbed her.

He was a little surprised she was sticking around.

She'd been hesitant at first, quiet. But then as Ryan hammed around with Ashley—who bore it somewhat patiently—she'd first cracked a smile, and then giggled behind her hand, though he saw her considering expression more than once.

They'd finished making what seemed like a thousand tacos and then joined the noisy chaos in the multipurpose room. It was a full house tonight, forcing them to squeeze in. His knee bumped Lila's under the table. Maybe on purpose.

She didn't seem to notice as she grappled with an over-filled taco. Every time she lifted it toward her mouth, some of the meat or lettuce fell out.

Finally, she stopped trying to stuff everything back in and just ate a bite.

She must've sensed his perusal, because she lifted her napkin to cover her mouth when she spoke. "There's no polite way to do this."

He made an exaggerated glance around the room. "I don't think they care about being polite."

But it was obvious she did, because she got up and threaded her way through the tables and chairs to disappear into the kitchen. When she returned and slid back into her chair, she was carrying a fork.

"Really?"

There was a slight blush across her cheeks, but she made no reply.

"So what are you planning for Christmas? Going over to Anna's?"

She shrugged and looked away, but he hadn't missed that dark expression.

"You're welcome at the ranch, you know."

She wrinkled her nose at him. "Thanks, Mr. I-don't-even-have-a-tree. Not sure I want to eat a microwave dinner for my Christmas supper."

"Hey, for all you know, I could've bought a tree since you saw the place last."

"Did you?"

He hadn't.

Her gaze told him she saw right through him.

"Why don't you come out with me after we wrap up here? I'll decorate if you bring the financial binder so we can talk about it."

He could see her mind whirling behind her eyes. His gut pitched, threatened to reject the tacos he'd just scarfed. It would mean visiting the attic and Mia's boxes of decorations. Rekindling the grief that had dimmed in the last several months.

Since Lila's arrival in town had distracted him from it.

"Better not, cowboy." She stood, lifting her now-empty paper plate.

"Stay," he said to her back. He didn't know if she heard him over the noise surrounding them.

She didn't look back.

But she didn't head for the door. She dumped her trash in one of the receptacles in the corner of the room and struck up a conversation with two boys who'd already finished their meals.

Right before his eyes, she'd soon organized an intense game of HORSE—boys versus girls, naturally—and was right in the middle of it with the kids.

At one point, Ashley's dog rushed the basketball and Lila got knocked to the ground. Ashley whistled and the dog sat on its haunches.

Ben had stood up without realizing it. Ready to rush to her rescue?

Ha.

Thankfully, Lila was already sitting up, one arm hooked over the dog's neck as Ashley approached and squatted beside her.

Lila was laughing.

Their eyes caught and held. He couldn't look away from her exuberant joy. She blinked when one of the teen boys came up and demanded the ball and the connection was broken.

He should grab her and demand they finish—start—talking about the ranch.

It seemed as if every time he started a serious conversation with her, she distracted him. Or ran off.

He shouldn't be intrigued. And in fact, he was annoyed. But a bigger part of him wanted to know her.

Know why she'd cried when she'd rescued that horse. Why she didn't want to step foot inside her home.

Maybe she was waiting for him to open up first.

Which meant he'd have to tell her about Mia, and he didn't know if he could do that.

CHAPTER 6

en hadn't seen Lila for three days. She'd been out to the ranch. Two of the hired hands had reported that she'd visited the mare every day—sometimes twice a day—but she always made a point to be there when he wasn't. How did she know when he would be gone?

He'd stared at that little origami tree she'd made him until he was cross-eyed.

The two suppers they'd spent together should have broken through the mistrust she'd had for him. He thought they'd started on their way to becoming friends.

Apparently he'd been wrong.

The sun was setting as he stopped in at the church for a final fitting of his Joseph costume. He hoped Lila would be here, but Velma informed him she'd had her fitting earlier, because she'd had to get over to the feed store where 'something was going on.'

He should have just let it go, but that had never been

his style, so after his fitting, he found himself turning his truck toward the feed store.

The stores lining Main Street were all blitzed out with garlands and lights, but he focused his eyes on the center line.

When he got there, the entire feed store parking lot was cordoned off with colorful flags and traffic cones blocking the entrance. Cars lined the street, and he was forced to parallel park. He set out on foot to find Lila.

And found her. She was driving a Zamboni in crazy circles on the parking lot, where a thick sheet of ice lay. Where in the world did she get a Zamboni? In Redbud Trails?

He ran into Ryan among the crowd of kids in colorful scarves and beanies, many of them lacing up ice skates. Although Oklahoma winters felt cold much of the time, it wasn't usually cold enough for ponds to ice over. Where had these kids gotten the skates?

Ryan was quick to point out a hastily-constructed booth across the parking lot, just behind the Coffee Hut booth. Both kiosks seemed to be doing a booming business, with a line stretching behind the building.

There was only one person who could be behind something like this.

Lila.

IT WAS impossible to ignore Ben once she caught sight of him from her place atop the Zamboni ice resurfacer.

She lost sight of him in the crowd as she drove the

machine off the ice and beside the side of the feed store. Then she caught herself straining to see him and forced her eyes straight ahead.

With three days of bitterly cold dry weather in the forecast, she'd had this idea and been unable to get it out of her mind. She'd always wanted an opportunity to skate outdoors in the winter.

Anna and Melody ambushed her as she adjusted her scarf, tucking it into the neck of her coat.

"Ben drove up," Melody said, her teeth chattering.

"I saw."

"You could do worse than a guy like him," Melody said.

She didn't know if her friend was forcing the issue—after Lila's multiple denials the other morning at their coffee date—to try and entice Lila to stick around Redbud Trails. If that was her endgame, her ploy was blatant.

Anna's eyes jerked to one side.

And of course, when Lila turned her head, Ben was there, appearing out of the crowd.

Before she could greet him or find out if he'd overheard Melody's remark, Anna's kids Mikey and Gina ran up and nearly bowled Lila over.

"Skate, skate!" they cried.

Gina tugged on her hand. "You promised, Miss Lila!"

And though Anna and Melody had faded back a little, Ben was still there.

Mikey noticed him. "You want to skate with us, Mr. Ben?"

"You can hold Miss Lila's hand with me," Gina offered.

His eyes came up to connect with Lila's, and she could see the fire burning him up.

The image of that ultrasound picture flashed in her mind. His baby?

Mikey glanced between the adults, maybe sensitive to the tension between them.

Gina, oblivious, walked right up to Ben and tilted her head up to see him. He looked down on her, and Lila wondered if he would put her off. The little girl crooked her finger at him, and he bent down to her level. She whispered to him behind her hand, and his eyes flicked to Lila.

He nodded gravely at the girl and when he rose, she took his hand.

"C'mon, we gotta get skates," Mikey said. He took Lila's hand and dragged her through the mob of people to the small booth where they asked for skates in their sizes. They found a spot where the crowd had thinned a little and sat on the sidewalk to shuck their boots and pull on the skates. Lila was intensely aware of Ben at her elbow. Why had he decided to join them?

And why was his presence sending thrills through her?

"I'm gonna skate backwards. Can you teach me, Lila?" Mikey asked.

She glanced over her shoulder at the makeshift rink and the people skating around it. "Maybe if the crowd thins out a little bit."

"You gonna teach me to skate, Gina?" Ben asked.

"No!" The little girl giggled.

"You never skated before?" Mikey asked.

Ben shook his head. His shoulder brushed Lila's as he tightened the laces on his skates.

"What about rollerblading?" Lila asked.

Another shake of his head. Negative.

"Rollerskating?"

Negative.

Why hadn't he just let them go ahead? What had Gina whispered to him that had made him agree?

Lila stood, balancing carefully on the edges of her skates. The kids did the same. Ben pushed up to standing, wobbling precariously.

"Whoa!" Mikey crowed.

Finally, Ben straightened out. They all four hobbled to the edge of the ice, where Lila was comfortable enough on her skates to help the kids and give Ben some basic instruction.

He caught on quickly, at least enough that the four of them could wobble around the edge of the rink together. The kids laughed and shrieked. Lila moved out in front of them, skating backwards but not showing off. She linked hands with Gina and pulled the girl along with her, laughing when Mikey bit the dust trying to catch up to them.

Mikey went off to skate with a friend. Gina linked hands with Ben on one side and Lila on the other. She chattered about a princess dress and a horse and more that Lila couldn't hear over the noise of their skates against the ice and the crowd.

And then Gina brought her two hands together, tangling Lila's fingers with Ben's. She skated to her mom, who caught her at the edge of the rink, leaving Lila and Ben connected and virtually alone, though many people skated all around them.

Heat suffused her cheeks as she glanced up at Ben, who looked down on her.

The toe of her skate must've hit an uneven patch of ice, because she suddenly wobbled. Ben's opposite hand came out to rest on her waist, connecting them as they came face-to-face. At least they were at a corner of the rink, out of the way of traffic.

She felt like a hundred eyes were trained on them.

"How'd you come up with this idea anyway?" he asked

"Maybe it was someone else's idea," she returned. "And I just executed."

He gave a slight shake of his head. He didn't believe her. "This has *Lila* written all over it."

She couldn't look away from his gaze. Something deeper was going on in his thoughts.

"How'd you pay for it?"

"None of your business." He probably thought she'd taken out a loan or blown a huge amount of money.

This has Lila written all over it.

Maybe it was spite that kept her from telling him about the two-day partnership she'd struck up with the skating rink two towns over. They were getting plenty of publicity from the stunt, and all she'd had to do was provide some manpower to help get things set up.

Let Ben think what he would.

But even as they separated and rejoined the main crowd, something niggled at her. She didn't want to care about his opinion of her. But she couldn't seem to help it.

THAT EVENING after the crowd had dispersed and Anna and Melody had gone—Anna to put the kids in bed and Melody claiming to have work to do—Lila found herself ensconced in the cab of Ben's truck, still on the curb where he'd parked.

They'd stopped to take off their boots and somehow, he'd convinced her to grab a coffee from the Coffee Hut when they'd turned in their skates.

Now a blanket of sparkling stars was spread out overhead, and everything had changed since she'd been in his truck the other night. He might've quit asking how she'd paid for the skating rink to come to Redbud Trails, but she needed to remember that *this has Lila written all over it* look in his eye.

"You've never had another job?" she asked as she sipped her black coffee.

"Been with your dad since I was fifteen, when my dad took the foreman's job."

That would've been just about when she'd left, but no matter how she searched her memories, she didn't remember a fifteen-year-old Ben. But then, she'd buried memories of those last days, and buried them for good.

And she couldn't fathom staying in one place for so long. "You've never wanted to do anything else?"

He shrugged. "I love the land. The animals. Working outdoors. I guess I was made to be a cowboy."

"I wouldn't think a true cowboy would be a mocha kind of guy."

He slanted a sideways look at her teasing words. "Well, this cowboy is."

She sipped from her plain decaf. "Haven't you ever wanted anything different?"

The question took them deeper than the teasing banter they'd shared since the near-spill on the ice.

Maybe he wouldn't answer. Thus far, their tentative friendship hadn't gone deep.

He considered her question, his gaze stretching far past the windshield. One of his hands rested on the bottom of the steering wheel while the other balanced his styrofoam coffee cup on his knee.

As the silence stretched, so did the tension inside her, pulling taut like a rubber band. She squelched it down, though she wanted to bounce her knee or tap her fingers on the passenger door.

"I had it," he finally said quietly. "What I wanted. All I'd ever wanted. Mia and I were ready to start a family. Then...she got pregnant."

He leaned his head back on the headrest, as if saying the words took so much effort that he couldn't keep upright.

And the tension that had been bubbling beneath the

surface all night took shape in the familiar coil, now wound uncomfortably tight inside Lila.

"We were ecstatic. And then we had an ultrasound. We were supposed to find out the baby's sex and instead..."

There was a part of her that wanted to block her ears. Ben had lost his baby first, then his wife? It was a testament to life's unfairness that a good guy like him would see so much loss.

The other, bigger, part of her hung on to every word of his story. "Instead...was there something wrong with the baby?"

His head rolled toward her, his gaze burning from the inside out, just like it had on the ice, playing with Mikey and Gina.

"The baby was healthy. But the ultrasound picked up Mia's ovarian cancer."

The coil tightened.

His head tilted so he was looking up at the dome light. "The doctors—all of them—pushed her to abort the baby. The cancer was aggressive, and the treatment she needed would harm the baby if it was still in utero."

"She refused," Lila whispered.

He ran one hand over his face, still gripping the coffee cup with his other.

"She refused," he echoed. "Said she'd bring the baby to term and then get the treatments. Only she didn't make it that long."

His voice broke near the end. The men in her life—

her father and others along the way—had all hid their pain behind a mask.

Ben wasn't like that.

Or maybe his pain ran too deep.

"She was a little girl," he whispered brokenly. He swallowed. "Emma Grace. I got to hold her, just for a minute."

To say goodbye.

He didn't have to say the words for her to catch his terrible meaning.

She watched the rise and fall of his chest, watched his throat work as he tried to gain control of his emotions. He still stared at the ceiling, and no tear ran down his cheek, though she could see his eyes glistening in the low light from the dash.

She sat helpless. Wanted to reach for him, but who was she to offer him comfort? A nobody. Barely a friend.

The coil wound tighter.

After interminable minutes, he reached blindly for his coffee. She caught his cup on the edge of the console when it would have tipped over, placing it safety in the cupholder.

He scrubbed both hands over his face. Cleared his throat. "Sorry. You didn't want to talk about serious stuff."

She hadn't, but it was a part of him. And she was scared to realize she wanted to know all of him. She *liked* him. Impossibly.

The realization was frightening, that coil tightened again, and she shrugged, now the one to look off in the distance. "It's okay."

A lone ice skater took the empty ice, moving faster than the others had, executing a graceful twirl.

She felt his gaze on her, felt his expectation, though she didn't know for what. For her to acknowledge his pain?

When the silence had become awkward, he cleared his throat again. "If you want to go over the ranch's financials, I can clear some time this week. I know they can be difficult to understand—"

Relieved that he'd changed the subject, she allowed her gaze to come back to him. He'd taken on the relaxed posture again, one arm along the back of the seat.

"It's okay," she said. "One of my degrees is in accounting, so..."

Surprise lit his eyes, pushed his eyebrows up slightly. "*One* of your degrees?"

So he didn't know everything about her. "I have three." Her nervous energy—she blamed the coffee—pushed her to tap her fingers on her knee.

"Let me guess. You also have degrees in... party planning"—he nodded to the improvised skate rink—"and sky diving?"

She snorted. "Nope."

"Family life?"

"Is that even a degree?"

"Marine biology? Art?"

She shook her head.

"I give up." He said it as though he didn't care, but the glittering intensity in his eyes belied his words. If Ben set his sights on something, he didn't give up.

She had to look away as the coil tightened again.

"Agriculture from UT, accounting from Colorado, and business management from Nevada."

Now he was considering her, his gaze probing deeper than she wanted him to see.

What had she been thinking, offering up something so personal?

Another impulsive moment coming to bite her in the butt.

"Sounds like you're ready for me to hand over the reins to the ranch anytime," he said in a slow drawl. "And like you've had a hard time settling down."

Then, he added the verbal punch. "Haven't you ever wanted anything different?" He parroted her question from earlier. "Like to come home?"

The coil sprang.

"I have to go." She kicked open the truck door and dashed for her Chevelle.

Even with miles behind her, between them, she felt wild and out-of-balance, out-of-control.

Because the truth was, *she had*.

CHAPTER 7

$\mathcal{T}$wo nights after the ice skating debacle, Lila found herself in another predicament.

She kicked the tires of the rental trailer but only succeeded in hurting her frozen toes. Even in the dark and through the swirling snow, she could see the wheel was ensconced in six inches of icy, slushy mud.

Because the truck was a rental, it didn't have any of the supplies a real cowgirl would've kept in her truck. Not even a cardboard box to flatten and shove under the tire.

Her equine passenger stomped his displeasure in the confines of the trailer, letting her know he wasn't happy with this situation, stuck on the side of the road in a trailer listing at an angle against the small embankment.

Well, she wasn't happy either. She was only five feet from the scene of her crime, and anyone who drove down this stretch of road could see them.

Probably.

Maybe.

The blinding snow obscured everything, matting Lila's eyelashes with clumps of white.

She got in the truck and slammed the door. Cranked the engine, which didn't really do much, because she'd discovered on her way out here that the heater didn't work properly.

If she didn't know how dangerous it was, she'd think the blizzard was beautiful. Especially if she were warm at home, curled under a blanket with a cup of hot tea. Watching a Christmas movie.

But no. She had to follow her stupid whims into another wild idea.

She sat in the cab of the truck, mittened hands on the steering wheel, questioning herself. Everything had gone wrong since she'd arrived in Redbud Trails.

Even if she wanted to unload the horse—which she refused to do given the falling temperatures and the fact that the animal had no shelter and no food—she'd cut the fence with wire cutters, so it was no longer capable of keeping the animal inside.

She glared down on her cell phone lying on the passenger seat near her purse. If the battery hadn't died, she could have called for help.

But not Ben.

Ben, who could somehow see through her to her secret desires.

Like *coming home?*

His words from two nights ago were blistered into

her brain, had been on repeat since she'd run away from him and his all-seeing eyes.

With no heat, she was out of choices. If she stayed here, she was going to freeze. She was roughly a mile away from the Circle A, if she stayed to the road.

Could she walk that far through the slicing wind and snow? Could the horse?

There wasn't much chance of getting lost. If she somehow wandered off the road, she would bump into her daddy's black plank fence on one side or the barbed wire on the other.

But she really didn't want to go to the ranch. She'd been planning to take the horse to Anna's place—but only long enough for her to devise a long-term plan for it.

After all, her time was short. The nativity started tomorrow. Christmas was in four days. December twenty-sixth, she would leave Redbud Trails behind.

She just needed to figure out what to do with the ranch in the meantime. She could give it to Ben. She could find a job anywhere. She didn't *need* it, and he seemed to love it. But it was Daddy's, her home. Could she really part with it? She needed to decide.

But first, she had to figure out how to get out of this latest predicament.

Was that Lila?

The headlights of Ben's truck cut through the curtain

of falling snow and swept across the dark pickup angled across the road.

He tapped on the brakes, careful of the deteriorating road conditions.

It took a minute for him to realize through the haze of snow that the white behind the truck was a trailer. If he squinted, he thought he could see the trailer's back tires sunk into the muddy bank.

When Anna had called him in a panic, unable to get ahold of Lila, somehow he'd known.

Well, he'd guessed.

This had been his first stop, but it wouldn't have been his last if he hadn't found her.

The figure inside the cab of the other truck didn't move. Was she hurt? Had the cold gotten to her already? His heartbeat quickened and adrenaline spiked as he slammed out of his truck and into the blizzard. He left the headlights on to see where he was going and rushed to her door, whipping it open.

She blinked up at him with owl-wide eyes. Snow swirled inside around him as he moved close, the wind buffeting the door to push against his backside.

He reached for her, one ungloved hand curling around her jaw and the other going around her waist as he hauled her in. She was warm to the touch. Not hypothermic.

Her knee bumped the steering wheel, and she uttered a muffled protest, which he ignored. He lowered his head and took her mouth. Relief sliced through him like the wind at his back as he kissed her lips, her chin, her cheek.

She looked more alert—and wary—as she pushed on his chest. She turned her head to dislodge his hand.

"Your hand's cold," she mumbled.

"It's snowing," he breathed into the crown of her hair, bowing his head to bury his nose in the sweet-smelling strands. "Why don't you have the heater on?"

"Doesn't work," she mumbled into his neck.

The relief that had swamped him moments ago dissipated and blew away like the flakes swirling outside the truck.

"Why didn't you call for help?" He shook her shoulders, just a little, so she'd know how badly she'd scared him.

He moved back slightly, and she ducked her head, her hair falling out of its braid and all around her face in a riot of curls. "My phone's dead."

She wouldn't have called before she was in trouble, that much was clear.

"We are going to have a serious talk." He pulled her out of her seat.

"What...?"

He pushed her toward his truck, squinting against the high beams he'd left on. "Get in and get warmed up while I see if I can pull this rig out of the ditch."

He followed her, catching her elbow when she stumbled once. Maybe she wasn't hypothermic, but her reaction time was delayed. Normally she'd have blasted him for his high-handedness.

He tucked her in the passenger seat and made sure the heater was on full-blast before moving to the back of the pickup where he always stowed emergency winter supplies.

He pulled out two value-sized bags of kitty litter, hefted one on each shoulder, and moved back toward the trailer.

He mixed one bag of the kitty litter with the mud in front of the tire as close as he could get it to the wheel, hoping it would build some traction into the transaction.

He was rounding the trailer when he caught sight of the three strands of barbed wire that had been cut and peeled back, creating an opening that bore hoof tracks and boot tracks. Small, feminine boot tracks.

Lila. What did you do?

He huffed an exhale, knowing this meant a long night for himself, and moved to pour the second bag of kitty litter in front of the other stuck tires.

He waved to Lila when he rounded to the front of the truck, just to let her know he was all right.

Inside her truck, the air was hardly warmer than it had been in the blizzard. It bit into his skin, and he shuddered. How long had she sat out here?

He spotted her cell phone on the passenger seat and some mistrustful part made him pick it up. Dead, just like she'd said.

He held his breath as he eased on the gas. The wheels spun. Spun some more. And caught.

He slowly pulled the trailer out of the ditch and onto the road, pulling up next to his farm truck, where he motioned Lila to roll down the window.

"Think you can turn around without getting stuck?" he shouted over the wind.

She smirked at him but nodded and quickly rolled the window back up.

His last glimpse was her sliding over the console to the driver's seat as he eased on the gas again and pulled the trailer out of her way.

He watched in the side mirror as she executed a beautiful three-point turn, keeping away from the ditch on both sides. When she was aimed the same direction he was, he led the way down the hill to the Circle A.

He took care to back the trailer as close to the barn as he could get it.

By the time he got out of the truck, Lila was at the rear of the trailer, already reaching for the door.

He took her elbow and forcibly towed her across the yard to the big house.

The fact that she didn't struggle told him how bad off she really was, even after being inside his toasty truck for several minutes.

LILA WAS STILL REELING as Ben pushed her inside the kitchen and pressed her shoulders until she sat at the nook table.

He'd kissed her.

The memory of those passionate kisses to her face and mouth played on a loop as she watched him unbutton his coat and then go to the cabinets and pull out a mug that he filled with water and put in the microwave. He rustled around in another cabinet until he pulled out a box with a brand she recognized.

He was making her tea.

He doused the tea bag in the steaming water and placed it on the table near her elbow, not realizing his kindness had sent a lump to her throat.

She was used to taking care of herself. Had been doing so for fifteen years.

She didn't know how to take the gift he offered her. Was a little scared of what it meant if she did.

He seemed oblivious as he squatted in front of her, first taking off her boots and then chafing her sock feet with his work-roughened hands.

Pinpoints of pain and awareness pricked the skin she hadn't even realized was cold as she looked down on the dark hair of his bent head.

Her fingers itched to reach out and touch it. She wanted to bury her hands in his rich hair. And maybe pull him up for another kiss.

Which was crazy.

He set her feet on the floor between his thighs and reached for her hands, first removing her mittens and then giving them the same treatment he'd given her feet.

Sharing his warmth with her.

Her eyes filled with tears.

She turned her head to the side, blinking furiously against the pricking, hot burning.

She could feel his gaze on her as he continued to work her hands.

He didn't say anything. Didn't tell her to suck it up or worse—try to comfort her.

Finally, he stopped, just holding both of her hands in his, his thumbs pressing into the back of her hands lightly.

"I'm going to go settle the horse."

"I can go with you." She started moving, restless with energy pulsing, but he squeezed her hands.

She looked at him, and their eyes connected.

"I'd like it if you would stay here. Get warm. Drink your tea. Trust me to take care of the horse."

He didn't make it a question, just stood, bussing a kiss on her cheek and squeezing her hands one more time before he buttoned up his coat and stuck his hands in his pockets for his gloves.

Through the window she could see him descend the three stairs off the porch and make his way through the blizzard with a strong, sure stride.

Still taking care of her.

BEN SETTLED the horse in the barn. While the mare—who still hadn't borne her foal—had made the transition well and was fattening up nicely, he didn't like the look of this one.

He made phone calls, first to the county sheriff to let him know what was going on, then to the horse's owner.

He offered the man an exorbitant sum of money for an animal in the condition this one was, and they struck a deal on the condition the man not press charges for Lila's actions.

Then he called the vet, but there was no way she could come out with the roads icy and blizzard still blowing. At best, she'd be there the next day.

After over an hour of battling the elements and making sure the horse had calmed enough not to hurt itself in a new environment, all he wanted was his dinner and his bed.

And maybe another one of those kisses.

He'd watched Lila's emotions seesawing as he'd worked to get her warm in the kitchen. He was a little surprised that he hadn't heard that crappy rental start up as he'd worked.

Maybe she'd smartened up and realized he was on her side.

Or maybe she'd been spooked by the snow after her near-freezing experience and was smart enough not to try to drive in it again.

She wasn't in the kitchen when he traipsed inside. This time, he took off his boots and left them on the rug at the back door. Took off his coat and gloves.

He washed up at the sink, wincing as the lukewarm water stung his skin. He splashed his face, wiped off with a nearby kitchen towel, and then just stood at the sink, gripping the counter with his head bowed.

He didn't know what Lila had been doing with that horse tonight.

But he did know she wasn't long for Redbud Trails.

He hadn't meant to kiss her. He'd been swamped with

relief and another emotion he was ignoring for the moment. Caught up in the moment.

She'd been his first kiss since Mia. And she mattered.

His heart was going to get ripped to shreds when she left.

But he still couldn't bring himself to regret it.

The house was too quiet. Had she somehow snuck back out to the barn? Or over to his place?

He did a sweep through the lower level before climbing the stairs. Norma was responsible for the big house, and the only rooms he ever ventured into were the kitchen and the office when he needed to do the books. In contrast to the complete lack of Christmas decor in his place, Norma had added tasteful touches like the pine swags threaded through the staircase's balusters and over the railing.

He'd never even been up here.

"Lila?" he called so he wouldn't scare her. His sock feet didn't make any noise on the wood floors.

Only one door stood open, halfway down the hall. He found her inside, standing in the center of the room with her arms banded around her waist.

A defensive posture if he ever saw one.

This must've been her room. Lacy curtains hung from the window, and posters of horses covered nearly all of one wall. The twin-sized bed had a floral cover and still had stuffed animals propped against the pillows.

It was a little girl's room. Or at least the bedroom of a girl who hadn't fully hit puberty yet.

Why had she stayed away for so long?

He wanted to demand answers, but when he stepped beside her, he saw the tear tracks on her cheeks, and something inside him broke for her.

"Ah, honey." He grasped her elbows and pulled her in, his arms coming around her back.

She'd run away from him in his truck when he'd mentioned *home*, but something had changed, because now she clung to him, her hands gripping his waist. She buried her face in his chest as she cried.

He didn't know what she was mourning. Maybe the lost relationship with her dad. Maybe the childhood that she'd lost. Maybe something deeper.

He just knew that he would die if he didn't hold on.

When her soft sobs had quieted to an occasional sniffle, she lifted her face to his.

He still didn't let go.

"Why are you still here?" she whispered.

He didn't know if she meant *on the ranch for all these years* or *here with me tonight*, but there was only one answer he could give.

He cupped her cheek and brushed a stray tear from beneath her eye with his thumb. "Because there's nowhere else I want to be."

He couldn't resist. He kissed her again. Deeper this time.

She responded sweetly, and joy swirled through him like the snowflakes dancing outside.

When his lungs threatened to burst, he tucked her close again, not ready to let go.

They stayed like that for a long time. Sharing kisses.

Him holding her when tears once again streamed down her face.

And in the wake of it all, one realization crystallized in his heart.

He might never be ready to let her go.

CHAPTER 8

*T*wo days after the disastrous rescue attempt, Lila showed up at the church a bundle of nerves.

The snowstorm had continued all night, and it had been late—or early, depending on how you looked at it—when Ben had left her to get some rest and gone back to the foreman's house.

She hadn't slept, not really, not with the house all around her, taunting her with its long-ago familiar creaks and groans.

So was remembering what things had been like before she'd made the biggest mistake of her life. Before she'd gotten her best friend killed.

Ben had come for her in the morning. Everything had been covered in a blanket of snow as he'd driven her back to her apartment.

If only the things she'd done back then could be covered over like that.

But she well knew that the snow would melt, leaving behind a muddy mess.

She had to tell him.

The kisses they'd shared had broken open something inside her. So had the multiple, long phone conversations they'd had in the two days since they'd seen each other last.

She was falling for the cowboy with the heart of gold.

But he didn't know about Andrea.

Mrs. Potts was in the church's makeshift dressing room, armed and ready to help Lila into the robe. After being out in the elements the other night, she'd worn two pairs of long johns beneath her jeans and three pairs of socks. Even though it had warmed considerably—to the forties—since the snowstorm, she would be standing outside for two and a half hours.

Mrs. Potts clucked as she tugged the fabric into place. "I suppose the folds of the robe will cover the extra layers you added." Although her voice rang with slight disapproval.

Two shepherd boys chased each other through the vestibule, ignoring Mrs. Potts when she called after them, threatening to phone their mothers.

And then Ben stepped through the door, cowboy hat in hand.

His gaze connected with Lila's, and her heart tripped.

She must've made an audible gasp, because Mrs. Potts patted her shoulder. "You'll do fine, dearie. We do need to take your hair down, though."

She tore her gaze away from Ben. With an effort. "What?"

"Your hair." Mrs. Potts tapped her tight french braid. "Let's have it down."

She felt more than saw Ben come near. "It's pretty when it's down."

She wasn't prepared for him to buss her cheek with a kiss or to squeeze her elbow. Neither was she prepared for Mrs. Potts to remove the band that held her hair in place or to start loosening the braid.

She was frozen in place as Ben said something and the older woman laughed, fingers still in Lila's hair.

He slid his robe over his head and adjusted it. His shoulders still looked as broad beneath the brown linen, though he looked a little self-conscious as he caught her staring.

He winked.

And the coil that had started tightening in her stomach loosened.

"Miss Velma, Miss Velma!" A little girl in a white costume with a pipe cleaner halo wobbling above her head ran up to them. "Eddie put a lamb in the kindie-garten class!"

Mrs. Potts allowed herself to be dragged away, calling over her shoulder for Lila and Ben to be in place in ten minutes.

And then they were alone, Ben looked down on her. He lifted one hand to play with the curls bouncing near her chin.

"I like your hair down."

He was close, but not quite in kissing range.

And what was she thinking? There were impression-able young children—and livestock—running around. Even though none were in sight right at this moment.

"It's crazy," she admitted. "That's why I keep it up."

"Curly," he countered.

"Unmanageable."

He tugged on the curl, his knuckle inadvertently brushing her jaw. Had he stepped closer?

"It makes me wonder what else you try to manage that won't behave."

Her life.

"It also reminds me of what happened the last time it was down."

His lips brushed her jaw where his fingers had been a moment ago, and surely this was no mistake, but before she could turn her head and meet his kiss, he backed away. "We'd better get out there."

She followed him to the side of the building that faced Second Street. The men of the church had constructed a barnyard scene complete with hay spread across the lawn, a manger, and a wobbly-looking pen where several sheep stood in a huddle.

Behind two hay bales someone had rigged heaters to blow onto the actors. It wouldn't be the same as being indoors, but it was a good counter measure to the cool night temperatures.

There were already bystanders on the sidewalk watching as they took their places in the scene.

Three shepherd boys ran out and stood behind the sheep pen, laughing and horsing around.

Lila felt terribly self-conscious. Were they really supposed to stand here for hours while people just *watched* them? Who had thought this was a good idea?

She must have muttered the thought, because Ben's lips twitched.

"You're a hard woman to pin down," he murmured. "I won't mind standing next to you for awhile. It'll give us a chance to talk."

She supposed if they kept their voices low enough, people watching them from several yards away on the sidewalk would never know what they talked about.

She swallowed hard. "I guess we could talk about the ranch finances."

His eyes sparkled, as if he knew that was an easier topic for her than, say, the reason she'd broken down and sobbed all over him the other night.

Or the kisses.

She definitely wasn't ready to talk about the kisses yet.

A young woman approached, a baby on her hip.

"I'm April. And this is Wyatt."

Lila's mouth opened, but no sound came out. No. Mrs. Potts wouldn't have stuck them with a baby.

Then again, what would the nativity be without the baby Jesus?

Ben smoothed over her awkward silence with introductions.

"Wyatt is almost nine months old," April said. "So not a newborn, but it is a little cold for a newborn to be out."

She looked at Lila expectantly, but Lila held up her hands in front of her in the universal sign for *no stinkin' way*. She didn't know anything about babies.

Ben reached for him instead, and the little boy snuggled right into the crook of his arm.

Which left Lila to receive the diaper bag April thrust at her. "He might get hungry. He can have a snack, it's right in here. His dad and I will be watching—and probably taking pictures—from over there." She motioned to the sidewalk, then left them with her baby.

Lila stowed the bag behind a bale of hay where she hoped it would be out of sight from the sidewalk.

Wyatt gurgled as he tugged on Ben's robe, then reached up to honk Ben's nose.

Ben only chuckled, moving the tyke's hand and then ruffling his hair. "I've seen you in services before, haven't I, buddy?"

"Stand closer, Lila—I mean, Mary!" Mrs. Potts yelled from behind the growing pack of spectators on the sidewalk.

One of the sheep *baaaed*.

Lila's cheeks burned, but Ben held out his arm that wasn't supporting the baby, and she stepped into him, completing the circle.

"This isn't so bad, right?"

She couldn't tell if he was speaking to her or Wyatt.

Speak for yourself.

Every moment spent close to Ben made her want

things she had no business wanting.

He made more baby talk with Wyatt. Held her hand between their robes—although she didn't think they were kidding anyone watching.

Something had changed.

Between them.

Maybe in both of them.

When he looked down on the baby and looked at her, his eyes didn't burn. Not anymore.

And that coil inside her started tightening up again.

LILA WAS GONE by the time Ben had slipped out of his costume and made a bathroom run.

He wasn't real surprised, not after the way she'd reacted when baby Wyatt had made an appearance in their scene.

But that didn't mean he was going to let her keep running away. He figured he could go to her apartment and cajole her into going ice skating. Or getting a bite at the diner. Or...anything.

But he was waylaid in the church foyer by Melody and Anna.

"If you're looking for Lila, she's already gone," he said, intending to just pass them by. He picked up his hat from where he'd left it on a high shelf, out of the reach of small shepherds.

"We're looking for you," Anna said.

That stopped him short.

"We're worried about Lila," Melody said.

Uh-oh. Was this the *hurt our friend and we'll kill you* speech? "Look, I like her. Really like her. I'm not going to hurt her."

Anna's eyes danced while Melody put a hand over her mouth. Laughing?

"That's good to know," Anna said.

"But we already figured that out," Melody added.

"So...?" What then? Was Lila planning something that could get her into trouble...again?

"She's still planning to leave after Christmas," Melody said.

"And we don't want her to go." Anna adjusted her scarf. "And it sounds like you don't either."

No. The very idea made his insides flip like flapjacks.

"We've got three days to figure out a way to get her to stay," Melody said. "Surely between the three of us..."

Anna nodded toward him. "I thought his vote counted double. He's the one she's falling for."

Her words sent him soaring. Was she really? Could it possibly be true?

He stopped his crazy thoughts. He'd done all that positive thinking after Mia's diagnosis, and that hadn't done him one whit of good. He'd been unprepared to lose both her and the baby, and the grief had nearly killed him.

He still held his hat against one leg, but now used the other hand to tunnel through his hair, letting out a gusty sigh. "I'm doing my best to reach her but Lila is..."

"Lila," Anna finished.

He'd been going to say *stubborn*. Or maybe

independent. Or even *hurting.*

"If you push her too hard, she'll run," came Anna's sage words.

"She's been running a long time," he agreed.

Melody's brows crunched together.

Anna nodded. "Ever since she lost her best friend, back in seventh grade."

"You knew her then?" He'd been a transplant, had arrived just before she'd gone away to boarding school. Arrived just in time to get his insides rearranged on her behalf.

Anna shrugged. "She was a grade younger than me. We weren't really friends, but in Redbud Trails, everybody knows everybody, you know?"

He'd been there long enough to know what she meant.

"She went a little wild when the accident happened, and then her dad sent her away. I don't know if she's ever really gotten over it."

She'd lost a friend. A best friend.

Knowing that, her tears—her grief—from the other night made sense. If she thought it was her fault... then her running, bouncing from place to place and never really landing, that made sense too.

Anna and Melody watched him expectantly, but what Anna had told him just gave him more questions—and no answers.

He and Lila had been butting heads since she'd returned home. And now he knew why.

What was he missing here? What hadn't she told him?

CHAPTER 9

*L*ila stood just outside the pregnant mare's stall. She was alone in the barn.

It was Christmas Eve.

Somehow she'd made it through two more nights standing next to Ben in the nativity scene, but where two nights ago, she'd experienced a ray of hope, now she just wanted it to be over.

And now it was.

Many of the folks in town had stayed to watch the shops on Main Street light trees they'd decorated over the last week. She'd seen Ben there, even seen him scouring the crowd for her, but she'd slunk away like a thief.

It hurt too much, standing next to his perfection.

She knew he would come back to the Circle A eventually, and she planned to be gone before then, but the mare's restless agitation had given her pause.

She'd seen enough live births before she'd left home

to know something was wrong. The mare had been up and down too many times. The hay was stained with blood.

And Lila's thumb hovered over the CALL button on her phone.

She pressed it.

Ben's name lit the screen first, and then the call connected. "Hey," came his easy greeting.

"The mare is foaling and something's wrong."

"All right." He said the words without even a pause, as if she'd been talking about the weather. His calm manner seeped through the phone and into her, allowing her to take the first deep breath in what felt like hours.

"I'm coming home. I'm almost there. Will you be all right if I click off and phone the vet?"

He hadn't questioned her. He'd just trusted her diagnosis.

That in itself sent tears to her eyes. She quickly blinked them away.

"I'm okay." Because of him.

He ended the call, and her mind began to whirl. There was running water, hot and cold, in a small washroom off the main barn. The vet would wash up there.

But she dragged several buckets of hot water and lined them up outside the stall anyway.

By the time she'd done that, Ben was striding into the barn, his gait sure and loose. His cell phone was still at his ear. He must still be on with the vet.

"She's gained a few pounds from where she was before. I can send you some pictures."

Send some pictures?

He clicked off and joined her outside the stall. His sharp eyes swept the pen, taking in the horse that had lain down again and the straw that had been stirred up by her movements.

"She's not coming?" Lila asked.

His arm came around her waist as if it belonged there. He pulled her close to his side and kissed her temple.

"She had an emergency call halfway to Weatherford. It's you and me." He squeezed her gently. "I'm glad you called me. Thank you."

She didn't know what to do with his gratefulness, so she didn't say anything.

He let her go and raised his phone to snap several pictures of the mare, then his fingers worked the screen as he must've sent them to the vet. In minutes, his phone rang, and he raised it to his ear.

"Uh-huh. Lila's with me. Will do."

He held the phone out to her. "She wants you to stay on the line. She's going to walk us through performing an exam and see if we can't help this mama out."

BEN LEFT his phone with Lila and rushed off to the small washroom in the barn, shucking his coat as he went.

He soaped up and rinsed off with hot water.

Then he stood for a long moment, just as he had in the big house kitchen days ago. This time, praying.

He and Lila had both suffered through more than their share of grief. She was on the cusp of running

91

again, and somehow he knew that if that mama horse died, he'd lose her.

And yet, he had no control of the situation. So many things could go wrong.

And how much worse could it get that this situation mirrored his own loss? Both mama and baby could die.

He had to find a way to get through this, for the horses and for himself. But mostly, for Lila.

When he returned to the stall, she was inside with the horse. She spoke softly into the phone, running one hand along the horse's neck. She must've been giving the vet more details than he could with his pictures outside the stall.

He'd pulled many a calf during his years on the ranch. This couldn't be much different, only so much more was riding on it.

"Um, she wants you to do an internal examination," Lila said softly from her place near the horse's head.

He nodded. The vet had gone over it in detail on the phone before he'd handed it over to Lila. He shucked his shirt, the cool air teasing the skin of his torso.

Lila's eyes flicked to him and away.

He approached the horse from the side. Its head rolled to the side, but she appeared to lack the energy to get up. Not good.

He touched her hip first, then slowly moved to where he needed to be.

His first thought was *it's hot*.

Lila relayed his concern that the mare might be feverish, but he lost concentration on her one-sided conversation as his hand slipped into the birth canal.

The mare's skin shivered just before everything clamped down on his hand and wrist painfully.

"Contraction," he gritted out. He had only a split-second glance to see her wide-eyed stare.

He relayed to Lila when the contraction eased. Then the tips of his fingers brushed against something soft.

Was that a breath against his hand?

He was out of room, more than elbow-deep inside the mare, stretching for just another inch.

"I think the cord is wrapped around one hoof." He grunted as another contraction took the mare, and he lost feeling in his arm.

"Can you get it unwrapped?" Lila asked, the phone dropped and forgotten in the hay as she moved to his side. Her hand brushed his shoulder.

"Don't know."

The vise released just a minuscule amount. He could barely feel his fingers, could only hope his brain was sending the right message to his muscles as he stretched... and his fingers curled around...

"Got it."

With a gentle tug, the cord came loose, and the hoof shifted into his palm. He brought it forward, past the foal's nose to its rightful place with the second hoof.

As another contraction bore down on the mare, he gave a gentle tug of both the hooves, and there was movement!

Within minutes, a healthy foal had been delivered onto its straw bed.

Chest heaving, relief rolling through him in a wave, he backed away, letting the mama, who moved with renewed energy, edge around to lick her foal clean.

Lila watched him from the opposite side of the stall where she'd backed against the wooden side, her eyes bright.

They'd done it. Together.

She picked up her phone and picked her way through the dirty hay around the mama and baby to join him.

He was covered in blood and other fluids and needed to make a run to the washroom.

"I'll be right back."

LILA FROZE as Ben turned to make for the washroom and she got a good look at his back.

The way he'd lain on his stomach, from where she'd been on the opposite side of the horse, she hadn't gotten a good look until now.

His back was scarred. A huge, ugly scar spiderwebbed across his otherwise unmarked skin.

The wound was low on his back, maybe just below his ribs.

And the past overlaid her present as she saw the teenage boy he would've been flying through the air after the bull had gored him.

No.

It couldn't have been Ben who'd saved her. She'd

wiped memories of that day, stuffed them down, and never examined them, even through spates of talking with grief counselors.

It wasn't him. She must be mistaken.

She was still standing frozen, just outside the stall, when he returned.

He was bouncing on the balls of his feet, like a little kid might. The joy of what they'd just accomplished shone through every pore, but she'd lost it.

She reached for that joy, tried to find it again, but it proved elusive.

"What's wrong?" He came even with her, reached for her hand, but she pulled back.

"Your—" She swallowed against the break in her voice. "Your scar. How did you get it?"

One of his hands came up to touch a spot on his stomach, just beneath his ribs.

Where his eyes had been open and warm just moments ago, now they were wary .

"You know where, Lila."

She shook her head, but there was no denying the truth.

"But, you—"

He reached for her again, and again she evaded him. He frowned. "My dad started here when I was fifteen. We'd only been on the place a week and a half, but I thought for sure you'd remember it was me."

She hadn't put the two together. She'd never known who the boy was who'd saved her, and she'd been shipped off so quickly that she'd had to leave that grief behind.

But Ben had lived with this pain too.

"How long did it take?" she asked. "For you to recover?"

He shrugged. "Awhile. What does it matter? It's ancient history."

The wound might be a decade and a half in the past, but it didn't change the fact that she'd caused it.

Just like Andrea.

CHAPTER 10

*L*ila stood in the barn for the second time on Christmas Eve. Almost Christmas day now.

She'd come back to the ranch to tell Ben she'd decided to sell. She'd handle the realtor from a distance. Find someone experienced in selling the whole property, cattle and all.

But all the yard lights had been on, and there'd been a commotion in the barn, and she'd never made it to the house.

The vet was there, and Lila's heart pounded painfully. Was it the mare? The new colt?

But Ben and one of his ranch hands were conversing outside the stall where he'd put the gelding they'd rescued—stolen—together.

"What's going on?"

Ben's head came up and the other man wandered away. When he caught site of her, he frowned, a muscle in his jaw ticking away. "Lila—"

He moved to intercept her.

Too late.

She caught sight of the vet bent over the gelding. The animal's mouth was covered in foam as it fought for what were obviously its last breaths. The vet was giving it an injection.

"No!"

Ben caught her as she lunged toward the stall door. He hauled her away from the scene and several yards down the corridor.

She beat his chest and shoulders with her fists, but he didn't let go, only held her tightly against him.

"Lila. Lila. He'd had pneumonia. He was too weak to fight it off."

She stopped struggling and rested her forehead between her clenched fists on his chest. "How long?"

"The vet diagnosed him that first morning."

"Why didn't you tell me?"

"Because we were treating him. There wasn't anything else you could do."

His grip on her had gentled. His hands clasped her shoulders.

Grief sliced through her so profoundly she was sure she was bleeding all over him.

She never should have come back to Redbud Trails.

"Listen to me." He shook her shoulders slightly, the way he had the night he'd rescued her from the storm. "This is not your fault."

She shoved against his chest.

He let her go.

"How can you *say* that?" she railed at him. "If I'd done something sooner, it could have made a difference. I drove off and left that animal in a bad situation."

"So did I. So did every other person who drives down this road. If anyone's to blame, it's the man who owned him. Who neglected him."

She knew that. Logically, she knew it. But knowing did nothing to assuage the pain of losing an animal that didn't have to die.

"We can't save everyone, Lila."

His words dropped into her consciousness like a pin dropping. It was as if the whole world hushed.

All she could hear were her own breaths.

BEN KNEW he'd said the wrong thing when Lila's eyes shadowed.

"Lila—"

He reached for her, but she pulled away.

How many times had that happened since they'd met? He made an overture, and she turned him away.

How many rejections could he take? Maybe it was a game to her, he didn't know.

She still didn't say anything.

"Honey, sometimes you just have to let go. Move on."

She nodded. "I think you're right. I actually came tonight to tell you I've decided to sell."

Her chin wobbled slightly on the words, but she jerked it up stubbornly.

He wanted to argue with her, but something held him

back. His intuition was screaming at him that there was more to it than this horse.

Maybe more to it than when she'd seen his scars and run off like a scared rabbit.

But he couldn't resist asking, "You sure you're not going to regret that later?"

She shrugged. Swiped at a fallen tear with the back of one hand. Her arms crossed over her chest like she was holding herself together. "I need to do that. Move on. It's been fifteen years. I can't live with this place pulling me down anymore."

He shook his head. "If it's about the incident with the bull..."

"That's only part of it," she snapped.

He shrugged off her defensive anger. "Maybe if you tell me the rest of it, it'll stop haunting you."

"I've had several therapists tell me the same thing." Her words were taunting, almost daring him to try.

But he saw behind the snappish anger to the wounded woman behind.

He sat with his back against a closed, empty stall. Patted the ground beside him.

He couldn't believe it when she actually joined him.

"My best friend was Andrea Patterson. We did everything together. Back then...she was the daredevil, not me."

He could see that. For all Lila's bluster and impetuousness, she was awfully OCD and logical.

"Her parents had a small spread. We both rode. Loved to race. That spring had been particularly rainy, and she wanted to cross the creek, but I saw how swollen it was, and I didn't want to."

She took a breath, and he heard how close the tears were. He wanted to reach for her hand but suspected she would only shake him off.

"She dared me and called me a chicken baby, and we fought. I begged her not to, but she did it anyway. Her horse got swept up in the current, and so did she."

He turned to face her, his bent knee nudging her thigh. "That wasn't your fault. Kids do stupid things."

"I should have stopped her." She said the words woodenly, staring straight ahead.

"If she was anything as stubborn as you, I doubt you could've."

She shrugged. "Then I should have gone for help. Been the tattle tale she accused me of being."

He shook his head. He wasn't getting through to her. Maybe her pain was too old. Too deep.

"So you've spent fifteen years reinventing yourself as an impulsive danger-seeker. Even though you prefer not to let your hair down. And you line up your dishes when you eat."

Now her gaze cut to him. She glared hard enough, he wanted to check and see if the ends of his hair had singed.

"How'd you really get in that pen with the bull?"

She looked away, her chin raising.

"You didn't know it was in there," he surmised. "It was an accident."

"It wasn't."

A tear trickled down her cheek and dripped off of her jaw onto the packed floor.

She inhaled noisily. "My dad didn't want to hear me crying. He sent me to my room. Told me to cut it out. That it didn't change anything."

He could believe it. Tom had been tough as nails. Good with animals but not with people. Nothing tender about him. Likely he hadn't known how to deal with a twelve-year-old girl's grief. He was probably even grieving himself.

"I wanted to die, too," she whispered, dragging him out of his memories of Tom.

What?

"I knew that evil old bull was in the pen, and I hopped the fence. Walked out into the pen, yelling at him to come get me."

He would never forget seeing her standing in the middle of the corral, arms spread wide. That stitch in time was blistered to his memory.

"But then you rescued me." She bowed her head, wiped at the tears that were falling in earnest now. "You tossed me over the fence like I was a sack of feed. I hadn't even seen you—didn't even know what was happening."

And he'd gotten gored by the long-horn for his trouble.

"And you were hurt...and that was my fault too."

He'd spent weeks in the hospital, months recovering from the internal damage that one horn had caused him. But he'd never regretted it.

"I'm *glad* I did it," he said firmly. "Proud to wear this scar if it means the world still gets to have you in it."

He hated thinking of her lost and alone back then. No one to turn to. Her father would rather she shut up than express the grief that must've eaten her alive.

"I'm sorry your Pop didn't know how to help you get through that grief, and I'm sorry he sent you away from a place you loved, but I'm not sorry about jumping in that pen. I'd do it all over again."

Her lips parted, and the disbelief in her eyes spoke volumes.

Because I love you.

The words stuck just behind his sternum. It was a heck of a time to realize it, when she was vulnerable, when something new had happened to hack at her grief.

Why would she believe him anyway? When she made it a habit to push him away and keep him at arms' length.

Instead, because he wasn't quite that brave, he said, "What happened back then doesn't change the way I feel about you. I'd like you to stay."

CHAPTER 11

*C*hristmas morning dawned bright and sunny.

Maybe some folks wished for a white Christmas, but Ben would take what he got.

He'd gone to bed frustrated, depressed. Lila hadn't responded to his admission that he wanted her to stay. She'd been quiet and reserved and bade him goodbye, leaving without another glance at the horse they'd put down. He'd watched her leave and wondered how he'd survive when she left for good. Then slept fitfully.

But this morning he woke with a sense of hope and determination.

She wasn't gone yet.

He had one more day to convince her to stay. And not just any day. Christmas.

Miracles happened on Christmas.

And maybe he'd stopped believing that when Mia died, but that was his own fault. It didn't mean miracles stopped happening. Just that he'd been unable to see them.

Lila needed a miracle.

And he was just the cowboy to give it to her.

So he got on the phone and started making calls.

SHE HADN'T BEEN at the apartment. He'd pounded on her door, even though her Chevelle hadn't been in its assigned parking spot. He'd waited in the cold for a half hour before deciding to take another tack.

When he returned to the ranch an hour later, he found her car half-hidden behind the barn, but she wasn't in the big house or the barn.

Which meant she was on the property somewhere on foot.

He saddled up two horses and set out to find her. She'd mentioned the creek when she'd talked about losing her friend, so that's where he headed.

He reached the stream and searched for her. He was about to turn away when he spotted her. She was sitting with legs crossed on top of a bluff overlooking the creek at its deepest point. Her brown jacket blended with the dry winter grasses, and her hair blew free in the wind.

Her hair was down.

He ground-tied the horses and approached on foot, his boots crunching in the dry grasses.

She didn't look up when he sat next to her, just stared out at the ice-encrusted water, sparkling in the late-morning sun.

He took her hand. Her skin was chilled. How long had she been out here? It couldn't have been that long, because he'd had folks coming and going all morning, even though it was a holiday. For his special project.

"I like your hair down."

It curled around her face and down her back, though not as wild as it had been when Velma had taken out her braid.

"You were right yesterday," she said softly, a catch in her voice. "It's time to stop pretending I'm someone I'm not."

He threaded their fingers together, a little surprised when she allowed it. "I like who you are."

She breathed out a huff through her nose, turning her face a little away from him. "I'm not as selfless as your wife was."

"It's not a competition. You're as different as night and day, but that doesn't mean I can't"—he stumbled—"have feelings for both of you."

He could feel her pulling away even as he hung on to her hand.

It was time to lay it all on the line. She deserved nothing less.

"I brought you a gift."

Now she jerked away from him, looking wildly around, though he was glad she didn't move any closer to the hill. He'd hate to see her tumble into that freezing water below.

He swallowed his fear and blurted, "It's my heart. It's yours. Whether you want it or not, you've got it."

She went still, her chin pointed away from him. She was like a greenbroke colt that had sensed danger, ready to run at the slightest provocation.

So of course he provoked her. "I love you, Lila."

Slowly, so slowly, she turned to face him. Her eyes searched his and gave him the courage to say the rest.

"I said it wrong yesterday. I said I wanted you to stay, but what I meant was..." He swallowed hard, but his voice still held a catch when he spoke. "Please don't leave."

She inhaled a trembling breath, and he stepped closer, reaching out one hand to her.

She stepped into the circle of his arms, and the cinch around his chest loosened slightly. He tucked her in close, brushed a kiss against her forehead. "Don't leave me," he whispered against the crown of her head.

He hadn't won her yet. He could tell by the tense way she held herself.

"It's time to come home," he whispered.

"I don't know if I can," she whispered back.

He hugged her closer, dropped his head so his chin was near her ear. "It's okay to be scared. If you need to grieve, I'll be here to hold you."

He felt her hands flex against his back. Like a colt that wanted to give in, wanted to stop fighting the bridle.

"Trust me," he whispered, squeezing his eyes closed and praying for all he was worth for his Christmas miracle.

LILA WAS in a daze as she allowed Ben to tug her toward

the two saddled horses he'd left several yards from where she'd been sitting.

She recognized the two geldings. She'd admired them when she'd been in the big barn.

She followed Ben, trusting him, all the way up to the palomino paint, where she balked.

Ben didn't let go of her hand. Her protector.

The man who'd taken care of her. Rescued her.

Loved her.

She didn't know if she could trust in his love. Did she dare?

"You haven't ridden since it happened," he said, and it wasn't a question.

She'd been bucked off of the horse of life and had never had the guts to get back on.

She wasn't like him. He'd lost his wife and their unborn baby, but he hadn't curled up in a ball and let life pass him by.

Neither had he stuffed his grief down and pretended to live.

He'd just lived. Allowed himself to grieve and then, to fall in love again.

How could she refuse to get on the horse?

She let go of Ben. Felt his deep inhale from feet away. He expected her to pull away, to run, because that's what she'd shown him.

Could she give him something different now?

She raised both hands and stepped closer to the palomino, allowing him to accept her scent, then touched the sides of his face.

He was a gentle soul, this horse. She could see it in his eyes.

She let her hands roam up his neck and down his back.

The motion was familiar as she tucked her boot in the stirrup and swung her opposite leg over the saddle. She settled in the seat. It felt so *right*.

But it also brought a cascade of memories and the sting of tears.

Ben pressed the reins into her trembling fingers, one hand lingering on her knee. "I'm right here."

Don't leave me.

The things he'd said to her, that had taken guts, especially since she hadn't given him any indication that she returned his feelings.

"I've got one more present for you. It's in the barn."

She'd been too grief-stricken to venture inside this morning, even though she'd wanted to check on the new colt and its mama. But with Ben beside her...

He mounted up, easily settling into the saddle. When he looked at her, he allowed her to see the warmth, affection, and yes, even love shining in his eyes.

They rode at a walk, side by side. Being here with him, allowing herself to feel the grief for Andrea, even her grief over the relationship she'd never had with her father, over the choices she'd made in the wake of her young life falling apart. It felt like, despite all the running, she was finally taking the first step to healing.

Maybe she would seek out a counselor again, talk things out.

In the yard outside the barn, he caught her hips in his hands and swept her off the horse.

Holding her loosely, he bent his head and captured her lips in a searing kiss. Before things could get too involved, he pulled back and brushed another kiss against her forehead. "I love you," he said again.

She wrinkled her nose at him, and he smiled. "Just wanted to remind you."

He followed her into the barn, the horses trailing.

She stopped short just inside the threshold. "What did you do?"

"Something impulsive."

Every stall had been decorated with an evergreen wreath. Every wreath sported a festive red bow.

"You decorated?" she asked.

"You should see my house. It's like Santa vomited all over the place."

Every stall had an occupant.

The sorriest looking horses Lila had ever seen. As Ben unsaddled and cared for the two horses they'd just ridden, her feet took her on a meandering walk up one side of the corridor and down the other.

The horses were under-nourished. Neglected.

"You rescued them?" she asked when Ben returned to the main corridor.

"Bought most of them, just this morning, from owners who didn't want them or couldn't care for them anymore. The sheriff gave me a list of horses that had complaints on them."

"This must be all of the complaints in the whole county."

He shrugged. "I figured I better use every weapon in my arsenal to get you to stay."

"We want you to stay, too."

Melody and Anna stepped through the open barn doors.

"What are you doing here?" Lila protested half-heartedly. "You're supposed to be with your families."

"Are you kidding?" Anna widened her eyes comically. "The kids were done with presents by seven a.m. And I've got Kelly watching over the turkey."

"You can't leave. Our girls' nights won't be the same without you," Melody said.

"And I think it's Melody's turn to fall in love," Anna said. "She'll probably need our help."

Melody laughed, a startled sound.

Lila hugged her friends, watching Ben over their shoulders. He stood with arms loose, open and ready to take on the world. For her.

"Did you tell him yet?" Anna whispered.

Lila shook her head.

"Then we'd better get out of here."

"Did you grab her car keys?" Melody asked Anna as they made for the door.

"I've got a wrench in the truck. We can steal her spark plugs."

"Don't touch my car!" she called after them.

Ben moved in close again, his hands coming to span her waist. "So?"

"So..." She tilted her head back to look up into his face. "Maybe I was too hasty when I said I wanted to sell." She tipped her head to one side. "It looks like I have a stable full of mangy, underfed horses that need caring for."

"And once you find them good homes, we can fill the barn up all over again," he offered helpfully. "But no more stealing in the night. Especially in snowstorms."

"Unless you're with me," she countered.

He narrowed his eyes at her. "Agreed."

She reached up with one hand and fanned her fingers across his jaw. It was stubbled, like he'd been in too much of a hurry this morning to shave.

"This is the best Christmas gift I've ever gotten," she whispered.

"The horses? Or me?"

She popped up on her tiptoes to brush a kiss across his lips. "Both. Can I stay?"

The last bit of tension bled from his shoulders, and he laid a passionate kiss on her.

"Wait, wait," she said with a laugh, pulling back from the kiss. "I want to tell you I love you, too."

His eyes softened, emotion clogged his voice when he said, "Good."

He hugged her tight this time, his chin resting on top of her head. "It's about time you figured out I was right."

ALSO BY LACY WILLIAMS

WILD WYOMING HEART SERIES (HISTORICAL
ROMANCE)

Marrying Miss Marshal

Counterfeit Cowboy

Cowboy's Pride

Courted by the Cowboy

TRIPLE H BRIDES SERIES (CONTEMPORARY
ROMANCE)

Kissing Kelsey

Courting Carrie

Stealing Sarah

Keeping Kayla

COWBOY FAIRYTALES SERIES (CONTEMPORARY
ROMANCE)

Once Upon a Cowboy

Cowboy Charming

The Toad Prince

The Beastly Princess

The Lost Princess

HEART OF OKLAHOMA SERIES (CONTEMPORARY
ROMANCE)

Kissed by a Cowboy

Love Letters from Cowboy

Mistletoe Cowboy

Cowgirl for Keeps

Jingle Bell Cowgirl

Heart of a Cowgirl

3 Days with a Cowboy

Prodigal Cowgirl

WYOMING LEGACY SERIES (HISTORICAL
ROMANCE)

The Homesteader's Sweetheart

Courted by a Cowboy

Roping the Wrangler

Return of the Cowboy Doctor

The Wrangler's Inconvenient Wife

A Cowboy for Christmas

Her Convenient Cowboy

Her Cowboy Deputy

NOT IN A SERIES

Love's Glimmer

How to Lose a Guy in 10 Dates

Santa Next Door

The Butterfly Bride

Secondhand Cowboy

Wagon Train Sweetheart (historical romance)

Made in the USA
Coppell, TX
22 October 2021